From deep inside the tunnel car sliding along the dirt. Edwin there," he said. They heard it again, a sound like dragging footsteps. "It's coming this way!"

Henry pulled his rifle off his back. Johann gripped his cross tightly and stared into the tunnel. As the shuffling grew closer, an important question occurred to him too late. Why would the Necromancer have a pit in the middle of the room where he tortured his victims? The only purpose it could serve was as a place to throw their remains when he was done with them, but there were no bodies on the floor, no bones.

A shape appeared in the mouth of the tunnel. Johann and the others backed away. The figure kept to the shadows, but pale white fingers, their nails crusty and black, gripped the stone wall at the edge of the tunnel. Edwin leveled his torch, and the flickering orange light revealed a boy in his late teens, tall, skinny, and as pale as fresh snow. His lips had been sewn together with thick wire. Slabs of metal had been bolted to parts of his flesh, and forklike tines covered his eyes.

"You poor child," Johann said, stepping forward. "What have they done to you?"

The boy grabbed Johann and wrapped his fingers around the priest's neck. His grip was as cold and hard as iron. The boy's throat bobbed as he tried to giggle.

Mystique Press is an imprint of Crossroad Press.

Copyright © 2016 by Nicholas Kaufmann
"(F)Earless" copyright © 2012
Design by Aaron Rosenberg
Cover by Dave Dodd
ISBN 978-1-946025-19-7 — ISBN 978-1-946025-20-3 (pbk.)
For information address Crossroad Press at 141 Brayden Dr., Hertford, NC 27944
www.crossroadpress.com

First edition
"(F)Earless" first appeared in *Still Life: Nine Stories*

IN THE SHADOW OF THE AXE

NICHOLAS KAUFMANN

For Peter Straub and Jack Haringa,
my favorite author and my favorite critic.
Special thanks to Daniel Braum, Sarah Langan, K.Z. Perry, Stefan Petrucha,
and Lee Thomas for all their help, Laird Barron and Ian Rogers for their
encouragement, and Alexa Antopol for her love, support, and proofreading.

CONTENTS

THE PAST THROWS A LONG SHADOW

AN INTRODUCTION BY LAIRD BARRON

The past throws a long shadow. Familial bonds can be indistinguishable from shackles in an ancient town such as Helmburg, Germany, circa the mid-19th century. The fog, like the fetid breath of a beast, comes stealing over valley and vale. Across the small, isolated town of Helmburg, lamps snuff as the midnight hour encroaches. Atop a mountain cliff, shadows cluster among the ruins of a castle. A thin red beam of candlelight flickers in counterpoint to the gloom of the village; a thin red beam that burns soft and cold in the highest tower and illuminates a winding stairwell, clotted with dust and cobwebs. One shadow stirs among the host. Indeed, the shadow stirs to purpose most damned, first lurching, then steadying to murderous intent. The shadow of shadows drags its axe down the many steps and out the yawning gate to a road that descends toward empty cobble streets, barred doors, and the low-burning hearths of restless dreamers...

Nicholas Kaufmann appeared on my radar during the early Aughts with his dark, dark collection, *Walk in Shadows*, and a pair of excellent horror/fantasy novellas, *General Slocum's Gold* and *Chasing the Dragon*. Both novellas were nominated for awards. Since those early days, he's written numerous stories and an urban fantasy series featuring an unkillable, but far from infallible, protagonist. There's a powerful emotional core in Kaufmann's work; he has real empathy for his characters—hero and villain alike.

This time around, his short novel plays an ambitious game within the framework of its homage to classic B movies and gothic literature. The narrative travels along parallel tracks—Black Easter,

1826, concerning the heroic actions of the protagonist's father and boon companions, and the current time, 1847, wherein an outcast son returns home to find much has changed in his childhood village, yet the shadow overhanging its populace is grimly, and inevitably, the same. Evil seldom recedes, it merely slumbers, awaiting the appointed hour to reemerge. The appointed hour generally coincides with one or more well-meaning fools who go searching for it, shovels in hand.

In the Shadow of the Axe is a tale that, like a magic lantern from days of gaslight yore, revolves and projects a blood-drenched, phantasmagoric tapestry of intertwined events/tragedies. It illuminates, in a muzzy and tantalizingly oblique fashion, the lives of the damned inhabitants of Helmburg. Chief among these is Kasch Möllhausen, a young ne'er-do-well who has recently been expelled from college and now flees home to his rural village of Helmburg, a bucolic setting marred by a dark history and the ruins of cursed castle Karnstock looming on a nearby peak—ruins that once served (and perhaps still do) as the lair of a vile creature referred to as the Necromancer. Alas, temperamental Kasch's own problems run far deeper than academic humiliation—his father, the village hero who once stood against the Necromancer, has suddenly died after years of drunkenness, leaving the boy alone in the world; most of the locals aren't particularly happy to see the prodigal son returned; and to compound these troubles, Kasch suffers from dramatic blackouts and is prone to fits of powerful, savage emotion that have culminated in violence. And now, a series of brutal killings is in progress. Does the Necromancer, that dreaded bogeyman of Helmburg, stir once more? Has he, or it, revived to visit bloody doom upon the land?

The novel came as a surprise when I first encountered the manuscript—while it possesses Kaufmann's familiar voice and attention to character, the setting and style are well-removed from what I've become accustomed to regarding his work. There's a potent sense of nostalgia here and yet the homage elements are redolent of a distinctly modern bent. In any case, a great deal of my affection for this story has to do with how it transports me to another time—not only to a historical rural Germany and its black forests and haunted ruins, but to the contemporary black forests and haunted environs of my own childhood.

I grew up in the 1970s and '80s—back in the American Cryptozoic when eight-track cassettes were the height of innovation and television/stereos gave you three channels. During the '70s, television networks shut down sometime after the late-late show with a national anthem farewell followed by a few hours of static. This was the era of black-and-white matinees and late-night monster flicks. Vincent Price, Anthony Perkins, Christopher Lee, and Peter Cushing were waning household names.

At the tail end of this era (around 1981), Cassandra Peterson, who often went by the stage name, Elvira, reintroduced adolescent boys of all ages to B movie classics via her *Movie Macabre*. Granted many of the films showcased by Elvira lived down to their provenance in the fevered and lurid imaginings of cynical producers and writers. There are gems, however. More importantly, the series framed these pictures in a way that raised questions (via Elvira's screwball and satiric analysis) and encouraged further inquiry into the genre niche.

I don't know if Kaufmann watched the shows I did, although we're from the same generation and commonality of pop culture experiences seems probable. Whatever the case, his book resurrects that particular time and place in a manner that adheres to tradition and is also profoundly meta. While unnecessary to enjoy the story, the meta aspect adds another layer of appreciation for those of us who loved *Movie Macabre*, old Universal monster flicks, and the lurid offerings of Amicus and Hammer films.

Kaufmann gives us the ghouls and goblins and supernatural trappings we horror fans crave. Yet, much like the best among those old pictures, he knows human drama is the real draw. Part of what makes his narrative successful is that aforementioned core of humanity he depicts so well—sons versus the ghosts of their fathers, the pangs of unrequited love, and the dreadful notion one can never outrun the long shadow of one's past. Most of us can identify with these things. Many of us are in pain; some of us are running.

Time is a ring of black blood flowing through itself. *In the Shadow of the Axe* imparts a lesson—everybody gets what's coming to them, whether they deserve it or not; and they always will.

—Laird Barron
Stone Ridge, NY
September 20, 2016

IN THE SHADOW OF THE AXE

1.

*T*here, do you see it? On the side of the mountain, rising from where the mist clings to the rock. All that's left of Castle Karnstock.

It wasn't always a ruin of crumbling stone. Before the assassins came, before the flames engulfed it, its turrets and towers rose proudly to the sky, the hallways echoed with the footsteps of its master, and the air trembled with the sighs of those called from the village for a greater purpose.

It may look dead, but don't be fooled. Castle Karnstock's heart still beats. Can't you feel it?

Can't you hear it calling you?

Don't you know me?

2.

Kasch Möllhausen opened his eyes, startled awake by a sudden, loud tapping. The coach bounced and shook around him as it drove over the bumpy terrain of the narrow mountain pass. He'd fallen asleep just after crossing the border into Germany. He wasn't sure how much time had passed since then, but if they were in the mountains they had to be getting close now.

The tapping came again. Kasch turned to the window. A blackbird was perched on the sill, its feathers greasy black as if recently dipped in oil, its eyes little beads of midnight. It pecked at the glass.

"Shoo," Kasch said. He tapped the window. "Get moving, blackbird."

The bird kept pecking, and for a moment Kasch had the panicked thought that it was trying to break through the glass to get at him. Something in those black, soulless eyes frightened him. He banged a palm on the window.

"Shoo, bird! Get!"

The blackbird fixed him with a single beady eye, then fluttered its wings and flew away, disappearing into the gloom of the flat, gray sky. Kasch sighed, relieved, and then laughed at his own foolish fears. The bird had probably been curious at the sight of a coach, nothing more. Coaches, he knew, didn't come this way often.

He looked down the craggy slope of the mountainside to the valley below and could just make out the shingled roofs, winding cobblestone streets, and outlying farmland of Helmburg, the village he hadn't seen in seven years. Not since he was thirteen and his father sent him out of Germany and across the Swiss border to a succession of cold, impersonal boarding schools, and finally, the university in

Bern. There'd been money for tuition, for room and board, but no letters, no visits, no word from his father in all that time. Kasch had been sent away, abandoned, and now he was returning in disgrace, a dog with his tail between his legs. Somewhere down in the valley his father waited. Luther Möllhausen, the Hero of Helmburg.

Kasch wasn't looking forward to this. The university would have sent a letter ahead detailing the troubles that led to his expulsion, which meant he would have no room to lie about why he'd come home. His father would demand an explanation, but what could Kasch say? He himself didn't understand what had happened. He'd had two good years at the university, high marks, always stayed out of trouble. He hadn't made any friends, but he was used to that after his lonely years at the boarding schools. Then a student named Otto Gruber had shown up. Otto, it turned out, was also from Helmburg. But instead of befriending the boy, Kasch grew to despise him. Otto was loud and dull-witted, and the sight of him receiving letters from home while Kasch's mailbox remained empty was like a knife twisting in his gut.

The university demanded physical exercise as well as mental, and fate had forced the two of them into the same boxing class. Put into the sparring ring together, something had snapped in Kasch's head. He blacked out, and when he came to, the teacher was pulling him off of Otto's unconscious body. The boy's face was bruised and covered in blood, his nose broken. His classmates claimed Kasch yelled vile obscenities at Otto while beating him, but he didn't remember that. He didn't remember any of it. Still, with the university's reputation at risk, the dean gave Kasch a week to pack his belongings and make his travel arrangements.

The coach jostled and bounced down the dirt road into the valley, pulling him from his thoughts. Before them, the towering iron gates of Helmburg stood open, as they always did. Legend had it that long ago, when the village was first settled, an old blind woman had prophesied on her deathbed that the gates would close only three times, and on the third Helmburg would fall. Helmburg had been a deeply superstitious village at the time—a trait it never truly lost—and the gates had been kept open by decree ever since. Only twice in recorded history had Helmburg been forced to close them—the first was when an army of French bandits had tried to take the village; the second was the year before Kasch was born, a day in 1826 they called Black Easter. Now, passing through the gates to the cobblestone street on the other side, Kasch thought he saw two more blackbirds perched atop them. He twisted in his seat for a better look, but they were already gone.

He leaned forward and put his face close to the window, taking in the village he hadn't seen in the better part of a decade. As far as he could tell, nothing had changed. There was the same tavern he remembered, Huetten's Bierbrunnen, and across the street was the apothecary shop, its wooden sign still sporting the diagonal, lightning-bolt crack that had been there since before he was born. He saw the Bürgermeister's house, its columned porch and marble walls no longer as big and intimidating as he remembered, and the constabulary building with its big iron bell out front.

And the church. The dark stone of its buttresses, spires, and belfries made the church look more shadow than substance in the twilight. No light came through the rose window over the door, or through the stained glass windows to illuminate the images of St. Peter and Daniel in the lion's den that he had admired as a child. A moment later, he saw why. Wooden planks had been nailed across its doors. The church was deserted. Everything in Helmburg was exactly as he remembered—except this.

When they pulled up to his father's house on the far edge of the village, he paid the coachman, then stood watching as the coach drove away into the blue-black dusk. Only when it was gone did he take a deep breath and finally turn to face the house. It seemed smaller, less impressive than he remembered during the first few years of his exile, when he'd pined so often to come home. The windows were dark. Kasch knocked on the door.

No answer came. He tried the handle, found the door unlocked, and stepped inside. "Hello?" he called. His voice echoed back to him through the pitch-black interior. He fumbled for his matches and lit one of the oil lamps on the wall. Its lone flame barely penetrated the dark. He lit all the lamps in the entrance hallway, brightening the room. "Father, are you here?"

In the light, he noticed a white sheet had been draped over the round mirror on the wall near the door. The sideboard beneath it was covered too. He walked into the sitting room at the other end of the hallway and lit the candles on the marble table in the center of the room. All the furniture was covered with sheets, he saw, as were the paintings on the walls. It was the same in every room he entered—beds, chests, dressers, chairs, all were covered. There was no sign of his father. It looked like no one had lived in the house for weeks.

He went back to the front door to get his bags. On the floor just inside the threshold, he found a single envelope that had been slipped under the door. It bore the seal and address of the university in Bern. The messenger must have delivered it while his father was away. That meant no one had seen it yet, no one knew he'd been expelled. He picked the letter up and carried it into the sitting room. There, he held a corner of the envelope to one of the candles and watched as the flames devoured it.

If anyone knew where his father was, it would be the people at Huetten's Bierbrunnen. From what Kasch remembered of his childhood, Luther Möllhausen had spent more time in the tavern than anywhere else, including his own house and the stables where he worked. Night after night he'd sit drinking what seemed like barrels of ale while young Kasch played hide and seek under the tables and in the cellar with Liese Maentel—Leelee, he'd called her then—the golden-haired daughter of Henry Maentel, one of his father's closest friends.

The dark streets leading back to the center of town were deserted and quiet, save for the grumbling of Kasch's hungry stomach. Only when he got closer to the main thoroughfare did he finally see other people. Men in frocks, waistcoats, and breeches walked beside women in buttoned-up caraco jackets and absurd bustles that made their bottoms look enormous. Kasch smiled and nodded at them, but they only glared back and quickened their pace. They didn't recognize him as one of their own. How would they, after so long? He was a stranger to them now, an outsider, and there was nothing less welcome in Helmburg than outsiders.

Light shone warmly through the windows of Huetten's Bierbrunnen, and the sounds of laughter, clanking steins, and tinkling silverware reached him on the street. Through the window, he saw it was packed wall to wall with villagers inside. He took a deep breath and tried to carry himself like he belonged, but the moment he opened the door the room fell silent and he was greeted with suspicious glares. He made his way toward the polished maple bar front that stretched along one wall, from the kitchen door all the way to the stairs that led up to the second floor. Villagers stepped aside and followed him with their eyes.

The barkeep, a bulky, mustached man whose suspenders strained to hold his pants over his big belly, eyed him warily. "I don't think I've seen you around here before," he said. "If you're looking for a room for the night, we have accommodations upstairs." He fixed Kasch with an unfriendly eye. "After that, I expect you'll be moving on in the morning."

"I have a place to stay," Kasch replied. "A house, actually. I was born in Helmburg." The barkeep frowned with concentration as he studied his face. Kasch held out a hand. "Kasch Möllhausen."

The barkeep's face softened. "Möllhausen, eh? Luther's son?" Kasch nodded. The barkeep grabbed a stein and pulled the tap, filling it to the brim with ale. "This one is on the house. Go find yourself a seat and the girl will take your order." Conversations started up again around him, and he could feel the tension drain out of the room. Kasch took the stein and was about to turn away when the barkeep spoke again. "I wanted to say…" He paused and pulled nervously at the tip of his mustache. "Well, I was sorry to hear, that's all."

"What do you mean?" Kasch asked, but the barkeep was already walking away to fill someone else's stein. Kasch took the last empty table, a small one by the door. He ordered a plate of sausage from a frantic, overworked serving girl who looked about ready to throw down her tray and storm out of the tavern. When she ran off to the kitchen, he watched the barkeep moving behind the bar front. Why had he said he was sorry? Sorry to hear *what*?

"You won't see your dinner anytime soon," a voice nearby said. A short, toadish old man waddled toward Kasch's table. "She might be back by dawn, but then again, she might not. May I?" He gestured toward the free seat with the beer stein he carried. Kasch nodded and pulled the chair out for him. The old man smoothed his white hair and sat, extending his hand. "Hahn Gehrig. I hope you don't mind, but I overheard you talking before. You're Kasch Möllhausen?"

"That's right."

Hahn nodded. "I knew your father. I'm so sorry."

"So people keep saying, but I don't know why."

Hahn furrowed his brow. "No one told you? Oh, child, Luther died two months ago."

Kasch's heart sank. The sheets over the furniture, no lights in the house—all signs he would have recognized right away had he not been so nervous about coming home. He cursed his foolishness. "How did it happen?"

Hahn nodded toward his stein. "The drinking finally got the best of him. He drank a lot after your mother Dora died, as I'm sure you remember, but after you left it got worse. One day he drank himself to sleep and never woke up. If it's any consolation, passing in your sleep is thought to be painless. Your father didn't suffer."

Perhaps he should have, Kasch thought bitterly. "I wasn't told of his death," he said. "I would have come right away if I'd known. Did they already hold the funeral?"

"Yes, shortly after he passed," Hahn said. "Your father was well loved by this village. Everyone was there."

"Everyone but me," Kasch said. They'd *all* forgotten him, it seemed, not just his father. They hadn't even thought to inform him of his father's death. This wasn't his home any more than the boarding schools or university had been.

Hahn took a sip from his stein and licked the foam off his upper lip. "And yet fortune has brought you back home anyway. I'm told there was some trouble at the university?"

Kasch took a deep drink of ale to mask his surprise, but he was sure his hands were shaking enough to give him away. He thought of the charred remains of the unopened university letter peppering the floor of his hearth, and asked, "Who told you that?"

"Fritz Gruber. His son Otto was at school with you, wasn't he?" Hahn shrugged. "Helmburg is a small village. Gossip is our only pastime."

Otto Gruber. He should have known. The dullard must have written home gleefully the moment he heard about Kasch's expulsion. But did that also mean everyone knew about his blackout, about what he'd done in the sparring ring? Kasch started to sweat. He quickly drained the rest of his ale and stood up.

"Excuse me, I'm going to go see about my dinner."

Hahn laughed into his stein. "It's still a good ten hours before dawn, my boy, but go if you must."

Kasch took a tentative step toward the bar, but there were too many people in the way, swinging their arms and spilling their drinks. He moved toward the kitchen, where they could wrap his sausage in paper to take home, but that path was blocked too. Behind him, four large, laughing men stood in front of the exit. Kasch felt hot, short of breath. The crowd was closing in on him, the smell and the noise. There was no way out. Darkness swam into the corners of his vision. The tang of ash filled the air. He'd felt this before, in the boxing ring just before he blacked out. If he didn't do something quickly, it would happen again.

Panicking, he spun around. A space had cleared between him and a yellow door set in the wall by the stairs. The door to the cellar. He knew it well from the games of his youth. Nothing was down there but barrels of ale and wheels of cheese stored in the natural cold. He'd be safe from the noise, the crush of bodies, the stifling lack of air.

He threw open the door and hurried down the steps to the room below. A single oil lamp cast a flickering light across the dirt floor. His heart racing, he leaned against a rack of barrels and let the cool, calming air wash over him. The voices from the tavern upstairs became a muffled hum. He breathed deeply, inhaling the sharp scent of cheese and the humid aftertaste of spilled ale. The darkness creeping into his vision dissipated.

Blackouts. Sudden bouts of panic. What was happening to him?

A voice came from the dark corner of the cellar. "You're not supposed to be down here. It's off limits to patrons."

A young woman emerged from the shadows, wearing a green dress with white lacing around the collar and carrying a bundle of sheets. Her skin was beautifully pale, like the porcelain dolls in the shop windows in Bern, and golden ringlets fell to her narrow shoulders.

"Leelee?" he said, surprised.

She frowned at him. "Liese, actually. No one's called me Leelee in years."

He laughed. "I should think not. You're hardly a little girl anymore."

She glared at him. "And who are you, exactly?"

"It's Kasch. Kasch Möllhausen. Don't tell me *you've* forgotten me, too?"

Her eyes widened, and she put a hand over her mouth in surprise. She dropped the sheets on a table and threw her arms around his neck. "Kasch Möllhausen, I can't believe it! You came back!"

"So I did," he said. The feel of her in his arms brought back happy memories of childhood games and the blissful glow of first love, and suddenly he didn't want to let go.

"I can't believe it's you," she said. She pulled away and looked at him, shaking her head. "And here in the cellar, no less. Your favorite hiding place. Some things never change."

Kasch laughed. "Not just for hide and seek. We had our first kiss down here, too, if I recall."

"Our *only* kiss," Liese said, and laughed. "We were just children."

"I didn't feel like a child at the time."

She picked up the sheets again and hugged them to her chest. "And then you disappeared on me. Left without even saying goodbye. It took me a long time to forgive you for that."

"It wasn't my choice. I didn't want to go." He looked down at his shoes. "Maybe we should change the subject."

"Maybe we should," Liese agreed. "Look at you, Kasch. You've grown so much."

"So have you."

"I'm told the passage of years has that effect on children," she said with a laugh. "But I always knew you'd grow up to be a handsome man. You remind me of your father that way."

"Now we really *should* change the subject," Kasch said.

"So you've already heard the news?"

Kasch nodded, suddenly uncomfortable, and looked back at the stairs leading up to the bar.

"I'm sorry," Liese continued. "Your father was a good man. A real hero."

He cringed. There it was again—Luther Möllhausen, the Hero of Helmburg. That he was also a drunkard who abandoned his son didn't seem to matter to anyone but Kasch.

He nodded at the sheets in her arms and asked, "So you work here now?"

"At the inn upstairs. Not very glamorous work for the Bürgermeister's daughter, which my father likes to remind me every chance he gets."

"Your father is the Bürgermeister?" Kasch remembered Henry Maentel as a well-fed man with a round face, neatly trimmed muttonchops, and a blustery way of talking without truly saying much—the characteristics of someone all but destined for politics. It was no surprise he'd ascended to the role of Bürgermeister. He had other memories of the man, too. When Kasch and Liese had been little, running around the tavern and playing their games, Henry and Luther had seemed inseparable, sitting at the bar front and talking in hushed, urgent whispers. Sometimes, he recalled, other men joined them as well. Kasch didn't remember who anymore, only that he was surprised sometimes to see Father Johann Vierick, the village priest, among them.

"My father has been in charge of Helmburg for five years now," Liese said. "He hates that I work here. He says it's beneath my station, even though the owners are family friends and I've been helping them since before he took office. I suppose he'd rather I stay home and receive suitors all day." She leaned in close, the fragrant scent of soap in her hair making Kasch's heart beat faster, and whispered, "I think I would die of boredom." A stray golden curl came loose from behind her ear and fell across her face, lightly brushing Kasch's cheek. She drew back with a laugh, tucking the lock behind her ear again. "Not that it's constant excitement at the inn, either. No one ever comes to Helmburg. But on nights like this, some of the patrons in the tavern like to sleep it off in the rooms upstairs. It's our busiest night of the year."

Kasch looked blankly at her. "It is?"

"Don't tell me you've forgotten the harvest festival?" she said, putting her hands on her hips in mock anger. "Everyone was out in the Rosenmann fields this afternoon for the slaughter of the oldest goat."

He shook his head. "The old superstitions. This village is stuck in the past."

"I don't know, there's something charming about tradition."

"Unless you're the oldest goat," he said. "You should travel more, Liese, see the rest of the world. It's eighteen hundred and forty seven, we're halfway to the new century. The whole world is changing, advancing, and Helmburg is still performing sacrifices in the hope that it'll bring a good crop year. They'd laugh at us in Bern."

"Let them," she said. "We're the ones with the good crops."

"Oh, I wish you could have seen Bern," he said. "It's beautiful. There's an astronomical clock tower with moving puppets that's hundreds of years old, and a zoo that's entirely comprised of bears. I felt different there. Free. I felt like I could do anything, *be* anything. But here I don't know if I'll ever be anything but Luther Möllhausen's son. I don't know if I even belong here anymore."

She looked sad for a moment, her sympathy writ large on her face. "I'll tell you what," she said. "I have the night off tomorrow. Why don't you come back then and tell me all about Bern? I'd like that. And in return, I'll tell you everything you missed while you were gone. Who married who, who broke whose heart, who was caught doing something awful with a pig."

"It's a deal," he said.

She stood on her toes and kissed him on the cheek. "I'm glad you're back, Kasch." Before he could say anything, she darted up the stairs. "Don't follow right away. If people see us coming out of the cellar together, they'll talk."

"Let them," he called after her. "This village could use some excitement."

He heard her laugh again, a warm, heartening sound he'd missed more than he realized. Then she opened the door, stepped out into the noisy crowd, and was gone. Kasch leaned back against the rack of barrels again. He couldn't believe it. Liese Maentel. Leelee. She was even more beautiful than he remembered.

When he returned upstairs, he found Hahn still sitting at his table. In front of Kasch's chair was a steaming plate of sausage, a small bowl of mustard beside it, and a fresh stein of ale. "Dawn came early," the old man said.

Kasch sat down and started cutting into the sausage. For the first time since his father had sent him away, he didn't feel worthless, abandoned, a disappointment to everyone. He felt happy. Actually happy. The future seemed full of promise, and maybe, just maybe, he could start over with a clean slate.

3.

Edwin Roebling made his way through the tavern's noisy crowd toward the door. He didn't mean to stare at the boy sitting with that cowardly old fool Hahn Gehrig, but he was too curious, and too drunk, to look away. He'd heard the boy say his name at the bar—Kasch Möllhausen. Luther's son. Even without hearing the name, he would have recognized Dora Möllhausen's features in the boy's face—the sharp nose, the high brow. And those piercing black eyes. Kasch Möllhausen, back in Helmburg. That wasn't good.

Kasch glanced up from his plate of sausage, and Edwin turned away quickly, pushing through the door and escaping into the fresh evening air. His shoes clicked loudly on the cobblestones as he began the long walk back to his house. His strength wasn't what it used to be, no sixty-year-old man's was, and the walk home from Huetten's Bierbrunnen seemed longer each time. Worse, it was a path he hated taking, but there was no other way for him to get home from the tavern without walking past that one uncanny, unnaturally white cobblestone.

The stone was fixed in its spot in the middle of the street, the same size and shape as its neighbors, yet entirely white for reasons no one understood. He knew, as everyone in Helmburg over a certain age did, that it had something to do with the Hillenbrand girl. What was her name? He cursed his aging brain, trying to remember. Ava. Yes, Ava Hillenbrand. The only victim to ever escape from the Necromancer. For all the good it did her.

He'd seen her the night she came back from the castle. The alarm bell had been sounding ever since Ava had been discovered missing from her bed at dawn. Most of the villagers were at the Hillenbrand house, trying to calm the girl's parents, speculating that she might have run off with a boy and would surely contact them soon. But in their hearts they all knew the truth. The Necromancer had taken her.

No one knew where the Necromancer came from, or even his true name, only that he'd appeared shortly after the kindly Baron Karnstock and his family disappeared, back when Edwin was just a boy. Then came the strange lights in the sky over Castle Karnstock, the empty graves, and visions of the dead. The Necromancer preyed on the village, taking one or two every year, children and adults who were never seen again.

Except Ava. She came back, and Edwin was the first to see her stumbling down the street in a daze, a nineteen-year-old girl still in her nightgown and bare feet. He'd grabbed her to keep her from fainting, called for help, and kept asking her if she was all right. Ava only stared blankly, her eyes big and round. A single drop of blood ran down her arm and landed on the street.

A gathering crowd had helped Edwin bring her home to her parents. Christian Hillenbrand, Ava's father, rubbed the girl's hands, her mother stroked her hair and told her everything would be all right, but Ava didn't respond or show that she understood where she was. Hahn Gehrig, who'd been the village doctor all those years ago, couldn't find anything wrong with her. There were no bruises, wounds, or marks of any kind. He couldn't even explain where the drop of blood that rolled down her arm had come from.

Ava's parents asked Father Johann Vierick to stay with her through the night and pray for her recovery. But by first light, everything had changed. Ava was dead, and Hahn had no explanation why. Johann wouldn't say what happened in Ava's room that night, and in the morning the cobblestone where that mysterious drop of blood landed had turned from charcoal gray to a stark, bleached white.

Edwin walked by that damn stone most every night. No one dared get close enough to replace it or paint over it, so there it sat, a reminder of Helmburg's cursed past. It still chilled him. To think his boy Frederick used to play with his favorite yellow ball on the very same street Ava had wandered, dazed and dying from—

Edwin shook his head and hurried on. He didn't want to think about what might have gone on in the castle. Frederick had not been as lucky as Ava. He'd never come back after the Necromancer took him.

When Edwin got to the corner, he thought he saw a figure sitting on the church steps. He paused, startled, thinking for a moment he was back on that awful day and Ava Hillenbrand was lurching blindly toward him like the living dead. But the figure stood up and moved into the circles of light from the oil lamps that lined the street, and Edwin saw that it was only Johann. He breathed a sigh of relief and tried to calm his foolish old heart as it hammered against his ribs.

"Edwin," the old priest said, staggering forward.

His voice sounded harsh and scratchy. Probably, he'd spent the day shouting at people again, Edwin thought. Everyone in Helmburg was familiar with Johann's ever-slipping grasp on sanity. Where once he wore the proud vestments of the priesthood, he now wore only stained rags, and seemed to prefer it that way. The only sign of the esteemed position he'd once held was the large silver cross that still hung from around his neck. Somehow, despite the filth that coated him head to foot, the cross was always shined and polished. That, if nothing else, was surely proof of the existence of miracles.

"Edwin, thank God it's you," Johann said, and grabbed Edwin's lapels. His breath smelled foul, and his cheeks and throat were carpeted with thick, dark stubble.

"Johann, let go," Edwin said. He tried to step back, but Johann's grip remained tight. He could have pried those fingers away with ease, but he didn't want to touch the man. He smelled like he'd been rolling in manure.

"It's louder than before," Johann insisted. "I can hear it in my head. I can't block it out like I used to. Not anymore."

Edwin sighed. "Can't block *what* out, Johann?" He had no idea what the man was raving about. He glanced away, not wanting to look into his wild eyes—the madness in them was too heartbreaking— and gazed up at the darkened church instead. He wished the diocese would send a priest to take Johann's place, but no one wanted to come to Helmburg. They all heard stories about the Necromancer and the priest who went mad, and they stayed away.

Still gripping Edwin's lapel with one hand, Johann pointed up into the mountains. "Why, the castle, of course. It whispers to me." He tapped his temple. "It speaks to me in my head."

Edwin frowned. He just wanted to go home. He clasped Johann's hand on his lapel. "Let go. It's time we both got some sleep."

"No one else believes me, but you of all people should!" Johann cried. "You *have* to!"

"Let go, Johann," Edwin repeated, louder this time.

A light went on in the second-floor window of a nearby house. The shutters flew open, and the wizened old face of Frau Nüsseler appeared. The elderly town gossip looked angry and disheveled, her white hair loosened from its usual tight bun. "Be quiet down there!" she yelled. Then she squinted at them. "Edwin Roebling, is that you? You should know better. You're not a child anymore. Off to bed with you!"

"Yes, Frau Nüsseler. I was just on my way," he said. The old woman closed her shutters, and he turned back to Johann. "Let go of me."

Johann sighed and released him, shaking his head. "No one ever listens. Soon it will be too late." He turned and walked away.

Edwin watched cheerlessly as the man who had once been Helmburg's priest, who had tended to Ava Hillenbrand in her final hours, who had proved himself as much a hero as Luther Möllhausen on that terrible Black Easter more than twenty years ago, loped off into darkness in search of a filthy corner to sleep in.

When Edwin got home, his wife Lotte was already asleep. She would yell at him in the morning, he knew. She hated that he'd been spending so much time at the tavern since Luther's death, and she certainly wasn't shy about telling him so, but there was no way she could understand the depth of the bond they'd shared, or the emptiness he felt now that Luther was gone.

He removed his shoes and walked softly down the hallway to his bedroom, passing Frederick's room. He paused when he noticed the door was slightly ajar. That was strange. He and Lotte had a silent agreement—the door would always be kept closed, the room unchanged from the last time their son had slept in it. Edwin pushed the door open and peered inside. Bright moonlight spilled through the window, illuminating the small bed, the chest of drawers at its foot, and the brightly painted wooden toybox against the wall.

In the center of the room, resting on the floor instead of in the toybox where it had been since the day he vanished, was Frederick's favorite yellow ball.

4.

BLACK EASTER, 1826

Edwin and Lotte Roebling sat in their usual pew in Helmburg's church watching Father Johann Vierick deliver his sermon on the Resurrection, but Edwin couldn't pay attention. The empty seats where Luther and Dora Möllhausen always sat distracted him. Where were they? It wasn't like them to miss Easter mass. He glanced across the aisle at Henry Maentel, hoping for a signal that their mutual friend was all right, but Henry was caught up in the service, nodding along with Father Vierick's words, one hand on his wife Carla's swollen stomach. Henry had told him they were hoping for another boy, one that would be like Abelard, the son they'd lost to the Necromancer.

When mass was over, Lotte practically pulled him down the steps outside the church. She was hungry and in a rush to get home, but Edwin hung back. "I should check on Luther and Dora, make sure everything's all right," he said.

"Don't be too long," she told him. "I'm not eating that whole leg of lamb myself."

He walked to Luther's house, wondering what he'd find. It was probably nothing, they'd overslept or were sneezing and bedridden, but still, it itched at him. Something wasn't right. When he reached their house, he knocked on the door and called, "Luther?" He waited for an answer. When none came, he opened the door and stepped inside. "Luther? Dora?"

He found Luther in the bedroom, sitting on the edge of the bed, a broad-shouldered shadow in the dark.

"Luther, are you all right?" Edwin asked. Luther didn't answer.

Edwin went to the window and parted the curtains, letting in the light. Luther's long hair and beard were a tangled mess, his eyes puffy and red.

"She's gone," he said, his voice cracking. "He took Dora. Took her right out of our bed. When I awoke..." He trailed off, his breath hitching, but Edwin didn't need him to continue. He knew the story all too well—the empty bed, the fruitless search, the lies he would have told himself that her absence was nothing but a misunderstanding, and then finally the horrible acceptance. Edwin had gone through it all himself when Frederick disappeared.

"I'm sorry, Luther." He didn't know what else to say.

Luther brushed his tangled hair out of his face. "I can't just sit here and do nothing while that monster does God-knows-what to her."

Edwin nodded. "I know. I felt exactly what you're feeling now. Angry. Helpless." He looked out the bedroom window. In the distance, Castle Karnstock sat like a blight on the mountainside. Their cross to bear. The ones who were wealthy enough to move away already had. The rest of them had no choice but to stay. And where would they go if they could? Helmburg was their home.

Edwin's gaze ran over the bed, searching for the blackbird feather that was always left in the victim's place, but he didn't see one. "Where's the feather? We have to burn it and scatter the ashes in water. You know the ritual."

"I'm going after her," Luther whispered.

He hadn't even noticed the wine bottle in Luther's hand until the man raised it to his lips. Edwin snatched it away. It was empty. Luther must have been drinking all morning.

"I'm going to bring her back," Luther insisted. "I'm going to kill him."

"That's the wine talking."

"We can't go on like this, never knowing who he's going to take next. It could be any of us. It's time we did something about it." Luther looked at the empty bed. "Long past time."

"You can't," Edwin said. "The Necromancer would kill you as easily as snapping a twig. He'd do worse than kill you. You've heard the stories, you know what he can do."

"Then come with me. Two is better than one."

Edwin shook his head. "Others have tried, Luther. None came back."

Luther glared at him. "He took your Frederick when he was just a boy, his whole life still ahead of him. Are you saying you don't want vengeance?"

"Of course I do." He sighed and sat down next to Luther. "I think about it every day. I imagine my hands around the Necromancer's neck. Squeezing." He shook his head. "We wouldn't stand a chance. We wouldn't even have the element of surprise on our side. He communes with demons and spirits. They'll warn him. We'll be dead before we get through the door."

"Not if we have more men," Luther said. "An army. We can take the castle and kill the Necromancer if we have the numbers."

"Let's not play this game anymore," Edwin said.

"Do you know what he does to the people he takes?"

"Of course not. No one does."

"Then how do we know they're dead?"

Edwin looked at him. "What?"

"What if they're still alive in the castle? Have you thought of that? What if Frederick is alive? What if *Dora* is alive?" Luther stood up and peered out the window at the castle. "We're going after them, Edwin. Help me round up an army, as many as you can. We'll need to leave soon if we want to reach Castle Karnstock by nightfall."

"Luther, this is madness."

"Do you want the Necromancer dead?"

"Yes."

"Do you want your son back?"

"Of course, but—"

"Then *help* me."

Edwin frowned. Was Frederick still alive? Was it possible? It was true they'd never found any corpses. The only one they knew was dead was Ava Hillenbrand. If the others were alive, if *Frederick* was alive, he couldn't just leave him there. What if his boy was suffering? What if he needed his father? Edwin looked into Luther's fiery eyes and nodded. "I'll help you."

They spent the rest of the morning going door to door, collecting as many people as they could. In the end, fifteen men, including Luther and Edwin, gathered at the gates. Not quite an army, but it was more than had ever risen up against the Necromancer before. Maybe they stood a chance, Edwin thought as his gaze swept the group. They'd collected torches and horse-drawn cartfuls of hay, dried twigs, and barrels of oil. Some carried muskets, others brought old swords and maces from their family armories. He saw Henry Maentel among them; Barend Lang, the tall, brawny constable; Christian Hillenbrand, Ava's father, his face so red with pent-up fury that it was almost indistinguishable from his bushy red beard; and, off to one side, Johann Vierick.

"Father Vierick?" he said, walking over to him. "What are you doing here?"

"I thought I'd better come with you. Someone needs to make sure the Lord grants us success," Johann said. He smiled, but it didn't quite reach his eyes, and Edwin thought he understood why. Johann had tended to Ava Hillenbrand. He'd watched her die. He wanted to see the Necromancer answer for that.

Edwin noticed Johann wasn't carrying anything but a worn, leather-bound Bible, its red silk bookmark hanging out of the pages like a tail. "We should get you a weapon, just in case," he said. "We don't know what we're going to find up there."

"I have all I need," the priest replied, patting his Bible. Then he reached into his boot and pulled out an old, chipped dagger. "But still, my grandfather's blade. Just in case." He flashed a quick smile at Edwin, who raised an eyebrow.

"You're full of surprises, Father."

The priest sheathed his dagger again. "It's an honor to die in God's service," he said, "but not a necessity."

A commotion rose in the crowd that had come to see them off. Edwin saw a short, dark-haired man pushing his way to the front. It was Hahn Gehrig, the village doctor. "What are you doing?" Hahn cried. "This is suicide!"

Edwin intercepted him. "Hahn, don't make this harder than it already is."

"It's madness!" Hahn shouted. "You'll be slaughtered before you make it halfway up the mountain. Don't do this. You can't possibly succeed!"

"We're fifteen men against his one," Edwin said.

"It won't be enough!"

"Then join us," Edwin insisted. "Make us one man stronger."

"I won't go to my death, Edwin, though you seem more than willing to go to yours. All of you. You've all gone mad!"

Edwin stepped closer, leaning into him. "You're a coward, Gehrig. If we fail, it won't matter to the Neromancer that you stayed behind. You'll die with everyone else when he takes his revenge on Helmburg."

"Then don't give him a reason for vengeance," Hahn pressed. "Stay here. Just leave it alone." Edwin shook his head at him and turned away. "Fine," Hahn said, "but I won't be the one to bury your corpses. Not this time." He stalked off.

Lotte grabbed Edwin's arm and pulled him to her, away from the others. "Don't listen to him." She kissed him, keeping her lips pressed against his for longer than she had in years. "Be careful," she said when she pulled away. "Be sure to come back to me. I'm not eating that whole leg of lamb myself, remember?"

"If I don't find Frederick—"

She cut him off with another kiss. "Come back to me anyway, Edwin."

As Luther began leading his small army forward through the gates, Edwin gripped Lotte's hand one last time. He glanced back and saw Hahn standing in the window of a nearby building, watching and shaking his head. Edwin took a bracing breath, let go of Lotte's hand, and followed the others onto the road that led to the mountain pass.

Behind him, the iron gates closed for the second time in Helmburg's history. The heavy *clang* reverberated through his chest. It sounded like the door of a tomb.

5.

When Kasch returned home from Huetten's Bierbrunnen, he found his childhood bedroom too small for him now and decided to sleep in his father's bedroom instead. All the furniture in the master bedroom had been covered with sheets, including the bed. He yanked them off and was surprised to see the bed was still made underneath. Exhausted and pleasantly tipsy from the ale, he stripped and fell into bed. It was more comfortable than the ones he'd slept in at the boarding schools and university, but at the same time, it smelled musty and he could feel the worn indentation of his father's body in the mattress. Had his father died right where he was lying now, sweating and sick, with no one in the house to hear his pitiful moans? If Kasch had still been living here, he would have heard. He could have done something. Instead, his father had abandoned him and died alone.

He rolled over, away from the indentation, and closed his eyes. As he drifted to sleep, he thought of Liese, the smell of her hair, the warm pressure of her lips against his cheek. Even after Hahn bid him goodnight, Kasch had stayed at his little table by the door, hoping she'd show up again, but she never returned from her duties upstairs.

In his mind's eye, he saw her standing before the silent, stoic beer barrels in the tavern's cellar, and he pulled her to him, kissed her just as he had when they were younger. He felt her hands on his bare chest, sliding over his skin. It lit a fire inside him, heated his blood, and made it impossible to sleep.

He opened his eyes and found himself standing before the bedroom window, looking out into the night. In the distance, silhouetted against the stars, the ruins of Castle Karnstock jutted out of the mountainside. Someone stood behind him—a woman, he realized, the soft warmth of her body pressing against his back. Her arm was around his shoulders, her hand on his bare chest. He looked for her face in the window's reflection, half expecting to see Liese in this shocking, delicious dream, but it wasn't her. It was a woman with honey-colored hair that flowed like a lion's mane from the widow's peak above her brow. She had a narrow nose, a small birthmark beside her wryly smiling lips, and almond-shaped eyes that seemed to draw him closer.

"Who—?" he started to ask.

"You never should have left Helmburg," she whispered in his ear, and the feel of her breath on his skin sent shivers down his spine. "You were an outsider everywhere you went. You felt it, didn't you? How they never looked at you as one of their own. You were different from everyone else, superior to all of them, and they knew it. They feared it in you."

"Yes," Kasch whispered back, or thought he did. He had a peculiar sense of duality, as if he were standing at the window but also still in bed. He could almost hear the measured sound of his own breathing, the feel of the sheets around him. Or was that only her arm, holding him close?

"You don't belong anywhere else," she said. "Only here."

He sighed and leaned back against her. "Tell me who you are."

"I have something for you," she said, and brought her other hand from behind her back.

6.

Edwin Roebling woke suddenly from feverish, confusing dreams. He couldn't remember them in detail, but the thick, anxious emotions they stirred up stayed with him into waking. Something about Frederick—but had that been part of the dream or a memory from last night?

He glanced over at Lotte. She was taking up most of the bed, as usual. She'd grown fatter over the years, and the woman who breathed steadily under the covers seemed almost twice the size of the woman he remembered marrying. He poked her, trying to get her to roll over so he'd have some room, but it was futile. She was asleep and dead to the world until morning. A lamb could be slaughtered outside their bedroom window and the noise wouldn't wake her.

He sat up and swung his legs out of bed. His throat was dry, and a full pitcher of water waited in the kitchen. Leaving the bedroom, he glanced quickly at the closed door to Frederick's room. The image of the yellow ball in the middle of the floor came back to him, but he wasn't sure if he'd really seen it or if it was part of his dream. He reached for the door handle, then stopped himself, shaking his head at his own foolishness. He turned and continued down the hallway. He needed water.

But more importantly, he needed a plan. If Kasch Möllhausen was back in Helmburg, he had to tell the others so they could figure out what to do. Kasch couldn't stay, that much was clear.

In the kitchen, the moon sent a bright, cold light through the window. Edwin grabbed the porcelain pitcher off the table and was about to pour himself a cup when a tapping at the window startled him. He looked up and thought he saw a blackbird sitting on the sill, but it was gone before his eyes focused. What he saw looking back through the window at him was a human face.

A boy's face.

"Papa?" the boy said. "Can I come in now?"

Edwin backed away from the window, knocking a chair onto its side and nearly tripping over it. He hadn't seen that face in decades. Frederick—yet somehow still just a boy.

"Please, papa?" Frederick begged. "I don't like it out here."

Hearing his son's voice again reawakened the hope he thought he'd lost years ago. He edged slowly back toward the window.

"Frederick? Is it really you? How…?"

But the window was empty. Frederick was gone, if he'd been there at all. Edwin slumped against the counter. What kind of cruel trick was his foolish old mind playing on him?

He sighed and turned to go back to bed.

Frederick stood in the kitchen doorway. His skin was so pale it practically glowed. His arms opened wide for a hug.

"No," Edwin said, backing away. "No, you're—you're not real."

"Papa, why would you say that?" The hurt in the boy's voice sent daggers into his heart. Frederick walked toward him. "Why are you frightened of me? Come hug me, papa. Don't you want to hug me after I've been away for so long?"

He was sleeping. That was it. He was sleeping and needed to wake up. Edwin shut his eyes tight, clenched his fists, then opened his eyes again. Frederick was still standing in front of him, arms out, waiting for his father's embrace.

The boy smiled and said, "Don't you know me?"

Frederick's edges blurred suddenly, and the boy was gone. A thick mist filled the kitchen. For a moment, Edwin couldn't see anything but gray. Then he thought he saw a figure, growing larger as it approached. Something shiny and silver sliced through the mist toward him, cutting off his scream before it left his throat.

7.

Walking the streets of Helmburg the next morning, the village looked smaller than Kasch remembered. Each side street off the main thoroughfare held less than a dozen houses, plus a communal stable and carriage house, all silhouetted against the wide tracts of farmland beyond. As a child, though, Helmburg had seemed enormous to him. He remembered walking with his father to his work as a farrier, or to the tavern at night, how it had all seemed an immeasurable distance, and the memory brought a pang of regret to his chest. He hadn't thought of his father's work in years, but watching him with the horses, shoeing them, trimming their hooves, had fascinated Kasch. Now, with the phantom smell of the horses in his nostrils, he remembered how he'd wanted nothing more than to be a farrier too. Life had been simpler then, uncomplicated by school expulsions, clandestine funerals, and vivid dreams of strange women.

He shook his head, still surprised at how real the dream had felt. Her arm around him. He'd woken alone and still tired, his sheets rumpled and wet with sweat.

Passing the church, Kasch looked up to where the buttresses, belfry, and tall stone spire groped upward for the sky, for heaven, for a promise of something better than the abandoned shell it had become. His foot hit something suddenly, and he tripped, falling and banging his knees against the hard cobblestones. He cursed himself for not watching where he was going, got back on his feet, and turned to see what he'd stumbled over. It looked like a mound of garbage, a pile of dark rags someone left beside the church wall. Then he heard a groan, and the rags moved. A gray-haired head emerged from the heap, arms and legs unfurled like flags, and an old man with a weather-worn face slowly stood up. The rags were his clothes, Kasch realized. A big silver cross hung around the man's neck.

"Where am I?" the old man whispered. His eyes found Kasch, and he backed up against the wall in fear. "Get away from me! Leave me alone!"

"I won't hurt you," Kasch said. "I didn't mean to kick you, I was distracted." He reached into his pocket and pulled out a coin. "Look, I've got some money with me, why don't you get yourself something to eat?" The old man eyed him with suspicion, as wary of strangers as everyone else in Helmburg. "It's all right, I live here," he explained. "My name is Kasch Möllhausen."

"Möllhausen?" The old man peered closer at him, and his lips curled into a sneer. "Yes, I can see your mother's face in yours, boy."

Something about the vagrant seemed suddenly familiar. Kasch glanced at the big silver cross again. "Father Vierick?"

The old man glared at him. "Just Johann now." He scratched at the flaking skin on his cheek. "There's no church, no Father Vierick, only whispers and shadows. And the castle."

Kasch remembered Father Vierick as an elegant, commanding presence in the church every Sunday, and a friend of his father's who sometimes sat with him at the tavern. Nothing like the man who stood before him. "What happened to you?"

"You shouldn't have come back, boy." Johann stepped closer. The foul stench emanating from his greasy rags made Kasch wince. "Luther didn't want you back. He knew." Johann pointed a bony finger in his face. "Bad things will happen. Bad things!"

Kasch frowned. "I don't know what you're talking about, but my father is dead. Have some respect."

"Luther sleeps with the others, back there," Johann said, nodding toward the stone steps that led to the cemetery behind the church. "All the heroes of Helmburg, now just food for the worms."

Kasch clenched his fists and gritted his teeth. "That's enough."

"I know of such things firsthand, boy. I saw them put Luther in his grave. You weren't there."

"No one told me. If I'd known…" He trailed off, unsure of himself. Even if he'd known, would he have come back to pay his respects to the father who had abandoned him?

"But you didn't know," Johann snapped. "He didn't want you to know. He didn't want you here." The old priest tapped his mottled forehead. "Think about it, boy."

It was clear Johann's mind was gone and he didn't know what he was saying, but that didn't mean Kasch had to listen to it. He turned and started walking away, willing himself to ignore the crazy old fool's words. Of course his father would have wanted him to come back for the funeral. Why wouldn't he?

"This whole valley reeks of death," Johann called after him.

"It's not the valley that reeks," Kasch called back. He glanced over his shoulder and saw Johann was already shuffling away, rounding the corner of the church and disappearing from sight.

Kasch kept walking until he reached the stairs to the cemetery, then he paused. His father's grave was waiting just down those steps. Was he sure he was ready for this? The part of him that was still angry wanted to turn his back on his father and keep walking, but it was a childish thought. You couldn't shame the dead.

What harm was there in paying a visit to the grave? If nothing else, he could say goodbye. Put this hurtful part of his past behind him.

He walked carefully down the old stone steps, and into the cemetery. The grass was spongy and wet with dew as he made his way around the stone monuments. Half the headstones were so old the names etched on them were no longer legible. He scanned the names on the newer stones, but none belonged to his father. Finally, as he rounded the base of a tall stone angel, he noticed someone sitting on the ground in front of a pair of cross-shaped tombstones. Moving closer, he recognized the old man from the tavern, Hahn Gehrig. The name *LUTHER MÖLLHAUSEN* was freshly etched into the first stone cross, and beneath the name, the date of his death two months ago. The second, older cross bore the name *DORA MÖLLHAUSEN*, his mother. Kasch felt a twinge of guilt, as he always did when he saw her grave. The date of her death was the same as his birth.

Hahn turned with a start and looked up at him. "Oh, you scared me, Kasch." He put a hand to his chest. "Never sneak up on an old man in a cemetery."

"Sorry," Kasch said. "I'm scaring everyone today. It's becoming a habit."

"I take it you've come to see your father?" Hahn asked. "I had the same thought after last night. Seeing you brought back a lot of memories. Your father and I weren't close, but I admired him greatly."

Kasch sat down next to him. The earth over his father's grave was still mostly bare, though a few small green sprouts of grass had started to grow. "What's to admire?" he asked. "He sent his only son away and never spoke to him again. What kind of man does that?"

"I'm sure he had his reasons," Hahn said.

"I wish I knew what they were." Kasch plucked a blade of grass and tossed it idly away. "I saw Father Vierick just now. Something's wrong with him."

"Now there's a sad story," Hahn said. "His mind slipped away over the years. It was gradual, almost imperceptible at first, but his sermons grew more outlandish and bizarre, his actions became more extreme, and finally we had no choice but to defrock him and close the church. We're still waiting for a new priest, but the bishop will never send one. Not to Helmburg."

"And you let him wander the streets and sleep outside the church?"

Hahn shrugged. "We couldn't lock him away, not knowing the man he used to be. So we tolerate him. But he's harmless."

"He said some cruel things. He said my father never wanted me to come back." He glanced over at Hahn. "That's—that's not true, is it?"

"I can't imagine why it would be."

"Sometimes I thought I was an embarrassment to him," Kasch admitted, his cheeks growing hot. "Sometimes, after sending yet another letter I knew he wouldn't respond to, I wondered if he had any love for me at all, or if he was too much of a coward to face his own son."

"If there's one thing I know about your father," Hahn said, "it's that he wasn't afraid of anything. He was the strongest, bravest man I knew. You know about the army of French bandits that tried to sack Helmburg?"

Kasch nodded. He'd heard about it many times. Everyone in Helmburg had.

"Your father was only a young man then, but he didn't waste a moment before joining the front lines to defend the village," Hahn said. "When his comrades fell, he dragged them off the battlefield without thought to his own safety. He took an arrow in the shoulder and didn't even blink. He just kept pulling the wounded off the field. He helped beat the French back with that arrow still sticking out of him. That's the kind of man your father was."

"With the arrow still in his shoulder?" Kasch scoffed. "You saw this happen?"

"Me? Oh no, I didn't go anywhere near the battlefield. I'm no hero. Your father had enough courage for the two of us, believe me."

"Then how do you know the story's true?"

Hahn gave him an offended look. "It *is* true. I was a doctor back then. I helped treat your father when he came back from the battle. I saw the wound with my own eyes."

Kasch glanced at his father's name etched into the tombstone, then looked away. His father could defeat an army of Frenchmen while grievously wounded, but he couldn't write a letter to his own son. "I didn't know you were a doctor," Kasch said, eager to change the subject.

Hahn grew quiet, and Kasch could see the old man's jaw clench beneath the skin. "Used to be," he said, "until I couldn't take it anymore. The blood, the pain. I couldn't stand to be around all that suffering." He stood up and brushed the dirt and grass off his pants. "I just wasn't built to be brave."

A blackbird dropped out of the sky and landed on top of a nearby tombstone. It squawked and fixed them with its beady eyes.

"Get out of here!" Hahn yelled at it. He stooped to pick up a handful of pebbles and threw them at the bird. "Go!" The pebbles rapped against the tombstone, and the blackbird took to the air again. Hahn watched it fly away. "Filthy creature. Bad omens, that's what they are."

Kasch stared at the old man. Everyone in Helmburg was crazy. That was the only explanation.

The deep tolling of a bell rang out, startling him. He stood and looked at the church at the top of the steps. "I thought the church was empty."

"That's not the church," Hahn said. "That's the alarm bell. Something's happening."

"We should go see." Kasch started toward the steps that led

back up to the village. He glanced over his shoulder and saw Hahn rooted to the ground. "Come on, someone may need help!"

Hahn's face was a mask of fear. He opened his mouth as if to make some excuse why he couldn't follow, then he sighed and said, "Fine, but we should really leave these things to the constables."

At the top of the stairs, a group of people rushed by, all hurrying in the same direction. Kasch followed them, looking back to make sure he hadn't lost Hahn, and soon found himself in a massive crowd gathered outside a white, tile-roofed house. Two constables stood by the front door, trying to keep everyone back. Kasch saw shapes moving in the windows behind the curtains, but he couldn't see what was going on. In a window at the corner of the house, a splash of red painted the glass from the inside.

He turned to an old woman standing next to him. "What happened?" he asked.

"Murder," she replied. She had deep lines in her face, and her hair was up in a tight bun. "Edwin Roebling is dead. And to think I saw him just last night, making all sorts of commotion in the street with that batty old priest."

Beside him, Hahn said, "Oh dear God, Frau Nüsseler, it—it can't be Edwin."

"Butchered in the dead of night," Frau Nüsseler replied, shaking her head and clucking her tongue. "Hacked to pieces, they say. To tiny little pieces."

8.

The blood that dripped down the window made Kasch feel sick and dangerously lightheaded. His breath came in short, shallow bursts. The crowd seemed to crush in on all sides. Blackness crept into the corners of his vision. His whole body tensed, his fists shook, and he knew the blood, the noise, just *being* there was triggering another blackout. The front door banged open—loudly, violently, multiplied a hundred times in Kasch's ears—and a group of men emerged from the house carrying something bulky wrapped in a white sheet. Red stains seeped through the linen. He said to Hahn, "I can't take this. I—I can't stay here."

Hahn's eyes were fixed in horror on the wet, unwieldy package. Kasch didn't wait for a response. Every nerve was screaming for him to get away. He turned and bolted from the crowd, the house, the thing in the sheet. He ran blindly down street after street, and when his legs couldn't carry him any farther, he stopped and leaned back against the brick wall of a corner house. Trying to catch his breath, he closed his eyes to the glare of the sun.

When the lightheadedness subsided, he opened his eyes again and found himself facing the wall. Somehow, he'd changed position without knowing it. A wet smudge of blood stained the bricks. A sharp pain stung his right hand. His knuckles, he saw, were bruised and bleeding.

Not again, he thought miserably. How long had he been standing there beating his fist against the wall? The sun hadn't moved far in the sky. Had anyone seen him? He glanced around himself nervously, but the streets were empty. Everyone was at the Roebling House. His secret was safe.

He tapped his forehead against the wall in frustration. When would he be free of this? Was his constitution really so delicate that the slightest bit of anxiety sent him into a blind, violent panic? Maybe his father had been right to send him away. He was pathetic. A disgrace.

Kasch walked the rest of the way home, cradling his bruised hand. When he reached the drive, a sudden, awful smell assaulted his nose. Then he saw the house.

Big brown crosses had been painted over the walls, windows, and door. Close up, the stench was overpowering. Even before he saw the clumps of straw stuck in the brown matter, he knew what it was. He recognized the odor. Horse manure. Kasch shook with anger. This was no harmless prank, he knew. It was a message. A warning. Someone wanted him to leave Helmburg.

He walked around to the side of the house. The vandal had struck there, too, painting manure crosses over wood, brick, and glass alike. One of the windows was broken where the vandal must have accidentally put his hand through. The shards, sharp as teeth, had small droplets of blood on their points. *So he cut himself,* Kasch thought. *Good, he deserved it.* Though it was nothing compared to what Kasch would do to the culprit himself when he caught up to him.

The sound of horse hooves on the drive brought him running to the front of the house again, thinking the vandal was back. Instead, he saw a horse tethered to the most ostentatious coach he'd ever seen, black polished wood with gold trim and thick red tassels in the corners. The coachman brought it to a stop right in front of Kasch. The passenger door opened, and out stepped a middle-aged man with a face as round as his belly, a bulbous nose, and a mustache that blended into the thick, graying muttonchops that grew on his cheeks. A tall hat perched on his head, and he wore a collared cape over his waistcoat.

Kasch frowned, annoyed. He was in no mood for visitors.

"Herr Möllhausen," the man said, fumbling to extend a gloved hand. He looked over Kasch's shoulder and gasped. "My God, what is this?"

"A welcome home present," Kasch said.

The man shook his head. "Obviously, this is unacceptable."

"Obviously." Kasch looked at the man's outstretched hand, then his face. Something about him looked familiar, but he couldn't place it. "I didn't catch your name."

"I'm sorry, forgive me for being distracted," the man said. "Terrible business over at the Roebling house. We haven't had such a monstrous crime in a very long time. My name is Henry Maentel, I'm the Bürgermeister of Helmburg."

"Ah, of course," Kasch said. "I remember. You were a friend of my father's." And he was Liese's father, he reminded himself. It would be wise to be on his best behavior, then. He forced a smile and shook Henry's hand, then winced in pain.

"You've hurt yourself," Henry said, looking at Kasch's raw knuckles.

"It's nothing," he replied, pulling his hand back. "An accident."

"Here." The Bürgermeister pulled a white handkerchief out of his pocket and passed it to him. "I won't take up much of your time. I just came to welcome you back to Helmburg and offer my sympathies, and those of the whole village, on the loss of your father."

Kasch wrapped the handkerchief gingerly around his knuckles. "Not the *whole* village," he said, looking back at his house. "Someone doesn't want me here."

"I'll send Inspector Lang over as soon as possible," Henry said. "As I'm sure you understand, he's rather busy at the moment. So am I, which is why we need to get this business out of the way as quickly as possible."

"What business?"

"I have papers requiring your signature," Henry said. "It's purely a formality, but the rights to the house and land have to be signed over to you. It's already yours by birthright, of course, but even with the laws of natural inheritance there are legal documents to sign." He smiled wistfully. "The world is changing, and with it the laws that govern men. That's what Edwin always..." He paused and cleared his throat. "I'm sorry. Edwin worked in the Helmburg law office. I—I just realized that was the last time I saw him, at your father's funeral. We'd been friends for a long time, we'd been through a lot together. But we were both busy men without much time for socializing. The years got away from us." His eyes unfocused again as he relived some distant memory. Kasch looked down at the kerchief around his knuckles, small spots of blood seeping through the white cloth, and he thought of the body in the sheet they had taken out of Edwin Roebling's house.

Henry turned to the coach and held the door open for him. "Please, it'll only take a moment, and then we can both be on our way." Kasch stepped inside the coach and sat down on the plush, maroon banquette. Henry sat across from him and released a small plank of polished wood from its catch on the wall, lowering it between them like a desk. He produced a handful of papers, handed Kasch a fountain pen, and told him where to sign.

The papers were filled with a frustrating legal terminology he didn't understand, but the longer he gripped the pen, the more his bruised knuckles hurt. Finally, just to get it over with, he signed his name. When he looked up, he saw Henry staring at him with a peculiar expression. "There's so much of your mother in your face," the Bürgermeister said.

"So I keep hearing. I never knew her." Kasch handed back the pen. "Are we done?"

Henry scooped up the papers, melted wax onto them and applied his seal. "Now we are. The house, the land, and all Luther's property are now yours in deed and responsibility."

Kasch glanced out the open carriage door at the manure-covered house he now owned, and sighed. "Can I ask you something, Herr Bürgermeister?"

Henry looked uncomfortable. "I really ought to—"

"Why didn't anyone write to tell me my father had died?"

Henry sat silently for a moment, his mouth a tight line. "I can't answer that question."

"You can't, or you won't?"

"Dwelling on the past will only eat you from the inside, boy. You can trust me on that. At your age it's best to think about the future instead, such as how long you're going to stay in Helmburg, and where you'll go from here."

Kasch leaned forward, not ready to let the matter go. "Did my father leave specific instructions that I not be contacted if anything happened?"

Henry shook his head. "I'm sorry, I don't have any more time for this."

"You were one of his closest friends," Kasch said. "You were together all the time. I remember it. You *must* know something."

Henry straightened and stuffed the folded papers into his inside pocket. "There's nothing to know. Take my advice and leave Helmburg. Forget this place. Forge a life for yourself somewhere new."

"Why? This is my home. Are you saying I don't belong here?"

Henry stared out the coach window, his mouth set in a hard line. "I have to get back to the constabulary. Edwin's body is waiting." He nodded curtly toward the open carriage door. "Good day, Herr Möllhausen."

More than an hour passed before Kasch finally lost his patience waiting for the Inspector to show. He found a scrub brush and bucket in a closet, filled the bucket with soapy water, and brought them outside. If the Inspector wasn't coming, he figured he might as well start cleaning the crosses off the walls. The stench was growing worse as the manure baked in the sun, and the odor had begun to seep into the house through the broken window.

Putting the bucket down by the doorway, he saw another coach pulling into his drive, this one much plainer than the Bürgermeister's. A man with streaks of silver running through his black hair stepped out. A jagged scar ran the length of his left cheek. He was a full head taller than Kasch and carried a blue cap under one burly arm.

"Kasch Möllhausen? I'm Inspector Barend Lang," the enormous man said. He stopped, and a smile creased his face. "My God, look at you. The last time I saw you, you were just a boy. You couldn't have been older than twelve or thirteen."

"Thirteen," Kasch said. "That's when my father sent me away to school."

Barend nodded. "That's right, I remember. But you don't remember me, eh? I'm not surprised. I had considerably less gray in my hair then. Besides, what boy pays attention to his father's friends?"

Another one, Kasch thought, and knew right away he wouldn't get any more answers from Barend than he had from Henry. Luther's friends were keeping his secrets.

Barend looked up at the vandalized house. "Is that horse manure? Who would do such a thing?"

"They're *crosses*, Inspector. Who do you think?" Kasch said as he led Barend around the house to see the extent of the damage.

"You don't mean Johann?" Barend said.

"This morning he all but threatened me. He told me I shouldn't have come back."

"Maybe you shouldn't have." Kasch glared at him, but Barend didn't meet his eye. He pointed at the shattered window. "Was this broken before?"

"No, I think it happened while Johann was…painting the house."

"We haven't established it was Johann yet," Barend said. "I've never seen him do anything like this before." He nodded toward the handkerchief wrapped around Kasch's knuckles. "What happened to your hand?"

"I hurt myself," he said. "Just this afternoon. A stupid accident." He smiled weakly.

Barend nodded and bent to pick up a shard of glass from below the broken window. "Not on anything too sharp, I hope."

Kasch's smile faded. "You think I did this? Why would I? What would be the point?"

"I don't think anything yet. My job is to assemble the pieces of a puzzle until the picture becomes clear." He dropped the shard. "Frankly, I'd rather be out finding Edwin's murderer."

"Fine, then just go so I can clean this mess."

"I'll ask around, maybe someone saw something," Barend said. They walked back to the front of the house. "Are you planning to stay in Helmburg long?"

"I suppose so," he replied. "I have nowhere else to go."

"Then I'm sure I'll be seeing you." Barend smiled without showing his teeth. It was the least genuine smile Kasch had ever seen.

A sudden commotion drew their attention. Seven men on horseback galloped down the drive toward them, raising clouds of dirt in their wake. Kasch shook his head. Why couldn't everyone just leave him alone?

The horses drew to a halt, and the men dismounted. Their leader came forward, a short man with a horseshoe of dark hair around his bald pate. The other six stayed behind him. They had heavy stubble on their cheeks, greasy hair, thick dirty hands, and practically vibrated with the threat of violence. Kasch almost took a step back, but held his ground. This was his house now. He could order these men off his property if he wanted.

"Herr Gruber, what is it?" Barend asked.

Gruber? Kasch stiffened. Was this the father of Otto Gruber, the boy he'd beaten bloody at the university? He fought the urge to take a step back again.

"It's that damn priest, that's what it is," the short man answered, his face red with rage. "Frau Nüsseler says she saw him all but attacking Edwin in the street last night, and now Edwin's been killed. Don't tell me I have to draw a goddamn map for you?"

"Let's try to keep a civil tongue, Fritz," Barend said. "You know as well as I do that Frau Nüsseler is an old woman who loves nothing more than to gossip and spread rumors. I don't even take her word with a grain of salt anymore. Now I require the whole bag."

"Johann's been causing trouble for years, and you know it," Fritz Gruber spat back. "Always harassing people, yelling about hearing voices in his head. Yesterday he cornered my wife on her way back from the market. She said he looked completely out of his mind. He grabbed her and said she was going to die, that everyone in Helmburg was going to die. She feared for her life, Inspector. We all knew he'd snap at some point and someone would get hurt. Well, someone's been hurt all right—someone's been hurt into little goddamn pieces. I wouldn't be surprised if that priest tore Edwin apart with his bare hands like the madman he is. And here you are, doing nothing while he walks around a free man, looking for his next victim. Who will it be, Inspector? You? Me? My wife?"

"A blade, actually," Barend said.

Fritz Gruber's jaw hung open. "What?"

"You said you thought Johann tore him apart with his bare hands, but in fact Edwin was killed with a particularly sharp blade. One that was either heavy enough or honed enough to shear through muscle and bone. Tell me, Fritz, have you seen Johann with a weapon that might fit the description? Or do you think he simply used his crucifix?"

"Who knows what he's got squirreled away?" Fritz said. "For all we know, he could have a whole basement full of blades under that church." The men behind him grunted in agreement. Kasch could tell they were itching for a fight and probably had been since the discovery of Edwin's body.

"And tell me this, Fritz," Barend continued. "Does he look strong enough to cleave through a man's bones? Perhaps all the liquor he drinks and garbage he eats is healthier than we thought. Maybe sleeping on the cold, hard street, open to the elements, has given him enormous strength and vigor."

"You're not going to do anything, are you?" Fritz growled. "You're going to let that damn lunatic wander free as a bird until he strikes again, all because he was a priest once, back before his brain turned to porridge." He shook his head in disgust and motioned for his men to get back on their horses. "If you don't do something about it, we will."

"Tell your blacksmiths to go back to work," Barend said. "Leave Johann to me. I'll talk to him."

"Don't just talk to him," Fritz said. "Lock him up where he belongs. I'll be keeping an eye on you." Then he turned to Kasch. "I'll be keeping an eye on you, too, Herr Möllhausen."

"Then it's a good thing you have two," Kasch said, trying to sound brave.

"Just watch your step, boy," Fritz said. He glanced over Kasch's shoulder at the manure on the walls and his lip curled in revulsion. "You're sick. You're as sick as Johann."

When everyone was gone, Kasch got to work scrubbing the walls of his house. The manure had hardened, and he had to work the brush hard to scour it off. It would have been much easier to clean hours ago, if he hadn't bothered to wait for Inspector Lang. And what had he gotten for his trouble? All but accused of being the vandal himself. Worse, he found himself agreeing with that blustering loudmouth Fritz Gruber—the Inspector needed to wake up and realize the old priest was dangerous.

Kasch had only arrived in Helmburg last night, and already it felt like a great weight on his back, weighing him down. The Bürgermeister's lies, Johann's harassment, the Inspector's false accusations, they all pressed down on him.

He worked his way around the house until he reached the back, where a narrow coldwater stream separated the house from the field he used to play in, now overgrown by neglect and blending into the woods in the distance. He dipped the brush into the pail again and started scrubbing manure off a window. He went gently, not wanting to break the glass and give the Inspector more reason to ignore the obvious and blame him instead.

When he reached the bottom of the window, he thought he saw something odd on the sill, half hidden by the spindly branches of a bush. He pulled the branches back to see.

Someone had carved a word into the windowsill. They must have done it years ago, he thought; the carving and the sill both shared the same weathered color. He traced the letters with his finger, and the weight pressed heavier on his back.

HURE, it read.

Whore.

9.

Night brought a heavy fog rolling down from the mountains, and with it a creeping anxiety that seemed to infect the entire village. Every face Kasch passed along the route to Huetten's Bierbrunnen was tense, on edge. Their eyes shifted nervously in his direction and they pulled their children away. Annoyed, he cut across an empty street to get away from them.

He was keeping his agreement to meet Liese at the tavern, a first date seven years after their first kiss, and yet he couldn't stop thinking about the strange woman in his dream. She'd been so beautiful, and so forward with him, touching his bare chest so shamelessly like that. Kasch was almost embarrassed that such a brazen creature had come from his own imagination.

Who was she? He didn't recognize her face. He must have conjured her from some discarded memory. Someone he'd seen at university maybe, or a window model in a shop in Bern. No, that wasn't right, it couldn't be anything so mundane. There was something special about her. He felt it. Something as personal and private as a secret.

A footstep behind him made him turn, but there was only the empty street. The streetlamps sent out smoky cones of light that glistened on the mist-damp cobblestones. He could feel eyes on him, but there was no one there, no movement at all.

When he reached the tavern, he put his face to the window and peered inside. It was as crowded as last night, but the villagers' expressions, the way they carried themselves, were different now. They weren't celebrating the harvest festival, they were drinking away the horror of a sudden, brutal murder. The hairs on the back of his neck prickled. This time he was certain he was being watched.

He thought he saw movement in a nearby alley, a shadow within the shadows. Just then, the tavern door burst open, startling him, and a young couple stumbled out.

Kasch slipped inside before the door closed again. He scanned the crowd for Liese and spotted her standing at the bar. Her back was to him, but he recognized her golden ringlets right away. He would recognize them anywhere. She was talking with another young woman, a redhead whose pale, ample cleavage threatened to burst out of the plunging neckline of her corset. Kasch worked his way closer but found himself caught behind a wall of drunk men waving for the barkeep. He was about to call Liese's name when he heard her friend speak, her voice shrill enough to carry over the din of the crowd.

"If I were you, I'd be more concerned, Liese. I mean, he was kicked out of school, right? Expelled for God-knows-what. Drinking too much? A violent temper?"

Kasch froze.

"Or what if he got a girl in trouble?" Liese's friend went on. "Did you stop to think about that? He might have a *child* out there, and if he does, you can bet he's going to marry the mother, not you. If I were you, I'd save myself the heartache and steer clear of him. I wouldn't even talk to him anymore."

"I know, Erika, I know," Liese said, nodding. "I don't know what I was thinking. He's been away for so long, it was just nice to see him again, I guess."

Kasch's hands balled into fists. A stocky, mustached man in suspenders bumped into him, spilling a fat drop of ale onto Kasch's shoe. The man watched the amber liquid in his stein slosh back and forth at the rim, then looked up. He blanched at the furious expression on Kasch's face and quickly moved away.

Erika put a hand to her bulging chest, as though she were shocked. "Nice, you say? How nice will it be to see him with the whore he knocked up at university, their little baby bouncing on his knee? Besides, he's only been away for a few years, not even *that* long, and look at all the trouble he's gotten into already."

"All right, all right," Liese said, raising her hands. "I get the point. My God, you're worse than my father."

"Oh, and did you hear about his house?" Erika sipped from a

small cup of wine and leaned forward. She looked positively ecstatic to have a new piece of gossip to share. "Crosses made of horse shit all over the walls. I hear he did it himself, just for the attention."

Kasch couldn't listen to any more of it. He stormed out the door into the street, heading back home. His blood boiled. The weight of this place felt like it would crush him. He couldn't believe Liese actually *agreed* with that meddlesome harpy. To hell with her. To hell with all of them. He didn't need anyone else in his life who thought he was worthless. There were plenty already.

His fate had been sealed years ago, he realized, the day his father sent him away. Kasch had begged him, clung to him and cried until his father forced him into the lonely coach, slammed the door shut behind him, and told the coachman not to stop until they crossed the border into Switzerland. All the resentment Kasch had kept bottled up since then, the blackouts and violence that led to his expulsion, he could trace it all back to that moment, the bang of the coach door cutting him off from everything he'd ever known. Just one more thing he could thank the Hero of Helmburg for. He hated this village and everyone in it. He'd been a fool to think he could start over here.

Lost in his anger, he didn't see a figure step out of the shadows until he almost walked into him. Kasch looked up into the scarred face of Inspector Barend Lang.

"Ah, good evening, Herr Möllhausen," Barend said.

"There's not much good about it," he replied. He remembered the footsteps he'd heard behind him, and the feeling of being watched. "Were you following me?" He laughed and shook his head. "Of course you were. Perhaps you expected to find me spreading manure on every house I passed?"

"Not you," Barend said. He looked around the street, but the fog had grown so thick the lamps could hardly penetrate it. "I was following Johann. He's been shadowing you all evening."

Kasch shivered. So the old priest had decided manure crosses weren't enough and was finally going to make his move. Well, Kasch would be ready for him if he showed his face again.

"I saw him standing outside your house earlier, like he was waiting for something," Barend said. "Turns out he was waiting for you. As soon as you left, he started following you. I lost him in the fog just now."

"Now do you believe me, Inspector?"

Barend shook his head. "I'm still not sure he's the one who vandalized your house."

Kasch stuck out his chin. "You still think I did it myself. Of course you do. Why should you be different from everyone else?"

"No one's accusing you of anything," Barend said. "It's just that I've seen children do strange things when a parent dies, act out in ways they normally wouldn't. Especially if the relationship was... complicated."

Kasch sighed impatiently. He just wanted to get home, go to bed, and forget this whole day had ever happened. "Then maybe you should tend to your own children, Inspector, and leave me alone." He expected that to be the end of it, but Barend only nodded sadly.

"I would if I had any," he said. "I never married, though I did have a fiancée once. Rebekah." He nodded into the distance, toward the ruins of the castle on the mountainside. "I lost her to the Necromancer."

"The Necromancer? I thought that was just a local legend."

"Oh, he was very real, I assure you."

"But surely the stories are exaggerated," Kasch said. "The man in the castle was a tyrant, a killer, but..." He shrugged. "There's no such thing as magic. There's no such thing as ghosts."

"Is that what they taught you at the university?"

"The world is changing, Inspector," Kasch said. "People are putting their faith in science now, in things you can touch with your hands. There's no room for the old superstitions anymore."

"I saw the Necromancer's power with my own eyes," Barend said, touching the scar on his cheek. "So did your father."

"He never spoke of it," Kasch said. "He wouldn't let anyone mention the stories around me."

"He was trying to protect you," Barend said. Kasch laughed at that. "I'm serious, boy. Those were dark times. Everyone lost someone, not just me. The Necromancer preyed on this village for decades. We were like cattle to him, nothing more. I was younger than you when he took Rebekah. We were picnicking in the Rosenmann fields. It was growing late, I can still remember how the sky darkened and the air chilled so quickly. I got up to pick some flowers for her while she packed up our things. I wasn't away long, maybe a couple of minutes. I didn't even hear a scream. When I got back, she was just...gone. On the blanket where she'd been was a single blackbird feather, the calling card of the Necromancer. I was devastated, enraged, but there was nothing I could do. Nothing anyone could do." He stopped, lost in the memory, and sighed deeply. "I don't know why I'm telling you this, except that I think it's important you know what it used to be like in the shadow of that castle." He glanced toward the mouth of an alley shrouded in thick fog, and his dour expression lightened. "Ah, there's our friend now."

Kasch saw the silhouette of a man in the mist. The light from one of the streetlamps glinted brightly off of something shiny and silver. Barend started toward the alley, and Kasch followed. The figure receded, vanishing in the fog.

Barend walked into the alley and was immediately swallowed up by the mist. Kasch paused, suddenly uneasy about following him in. The fog looked as solid as a wall. He took a steadying breath and stepped through. For a moment he couldn't see anything but a hazy grayness all around him, but as he continued forward, the brick alley walls materialized on either side. Then he saw Barend and Johann. The old priest was leaning back against the wall. Light reflected off the big silver cross around his neck.

"Show me your hands, Johann," Barend was saying. "Show them to me."

Johann squirmed, refusing to let Barend touch him. "Hands, hands," he muttered. "Idle hands are the devil's playthings. Sit thou at my right hand, until I make thine enemies thy footstool."

Drawing closer, Kasch flinched at the terrible odor. Johann smelled worse than he had that morning, as though he'd spent the day handling horse manure. "There, you smell it too, don't you, Inspector? I told you."

Johann backed away from Kasch. "No, not him!" He stumbled across the alley to the opposite wall and put his hands to his forehead. "Get him away from me. The voices, they—they tell me about him. They know his name." He hugged himself and started rocking back and forth. "They talk to me about so many things. I try not to listen, but they're so much louder now. How am I to know which things they say are real and which are lies?"

"Why were you following me?" Kasch demanded. "Why did you do that to my house?"

"Don't," Barend said. "It's best not to get him excited."

"Why won't you leave me alone?" Kasch pressed. His fists shook. Part of him wanted to strangle the crazy old bastard with the chain of his own cross.

"Blood!" Johann cried. "Blood all over you, blood inside you. Whose blood runs in your veins, boy? You shouldn't have come back! I told you bad things would happen!"

"Father Vierick," Barend said gently.

Johann quieted. A fleeting light of recognition broke through the insanity in his eyes. "B—Barend?" he stammered.

"Yes, it's me, Father. Barend Lang, your old friend. Let me see your hands." This time, Johann didn't argue. Barend took his hands and examined them. Kasch saw they were filthy and lined with dozens of small scrapes and cuts. "Where did you get these cuts, Father?" Barend asked. "Did you break a window by accident? Did you do something to this boy's house?"

Johann yanked his hands back and started walking away. "He shouldn't have come back. Tell him to go, Barend. Give him money and a horse, tell him to go and never come back." Then the old priest turned a corner and was lost in the fog.

Kasch glowered at Barend. "Aren't you going to go after him? You saw the cuts on his hands. You smelled him. It's clear he's the vandal."

"He lives on the street. He could have gotten those cuts anywhere. Same with the smell."

"Then at least arrest him on suspicion," Kasch insisted. "Maybe Fritz Gruber was right. He's crazy enough to do something dangerous."

Barend sighed, shaking his head sadly. "It may be hard for you to believe, but he wasn't always like this. He was a great man. We did something good once, a long time ago. Him and me, and your father, too. Something important."

Kasch sighed. He was getting tired of the deference everyone showed Johann when it was obvious the man was dangerously unhinged. "And what would that be, Inspector? What was so good and important?"

"We killed a man," Barend said.

10.

BLACK EASTER, 1826

The spring air on the winding mountain trail was colder than down in the valley, and the sky seemed to grow grayer and darker the closer Luther's small army got to Castle Karnstock. Barend Lang tried to load his grandfather's ancient, stubborn crossbow, but it wasn't taking. A loose patch of gravel slid under his feet, and he fell to his knees, losing his grip on the weapon. It bounced into the path of one of the horse-drawn carts, and before he could snatch it away, was run over by the front wheel. With a loud crack, the weapon's bow and tiller both snapped in half. The horse pulling the cart didn't even blink, only trampled forward indifferently.

Barend cursed and rose to his feet, brushing the dirt off his pants. He picked up a lone crank that had broken off the crossbow's pulley and regarded it sadly. "A family heirloom," he sighed.

Father Johann Vierick clapped a hand on Barend's shoulder and chuckled. "You can always hang back with me, where it's safer."

"Wonderful," Barend groaned. "And when they tell the tale of how we stormed the castle and freed Helmburg, they'll be sure to include how brave Barend Lang stayed in back with the horses."

"That's if we succeed," Johann said. "It hasn't been that long since Christoph Hellner and his brothers went before us. Two years maybe. They never returned. There's a good chance we'll follow in their footsteps, and the footsteps of everyone who ever tried to bring down the Necromancer."

"I knew Christoph," Barend said as they walked. "Our families were close. My sister and her husband had us over for dinner shortly before they left, me and Christoph and his brothers. She cried the whole time and begged them not to go. My brother-in-law, on the other hand, is much less emotional. He simply gave Christoph a Saint Joseph medallion for protection. For all the good it did. But we have a much larger group than the four Hellner brothers. We're better armed and better organized." He patted Johann on the back. "And we have you for our Saint Joseph."

Johann smiled mirthlessly. "For all the good it will do, eh?"

Under the low branches of a pine tree by the side of the path Barend saw a small wooden hutch atop a thick post. Sheltered beneath its peaked roof was a carving of Christ on the cross, his painted skin faded from wind and rain. Johann walked over to it, but Barend hung back, watching. The priest crossed himself and silently mouth a prayer. Then he reached out and placed two fingers over Christ's eyes.

"Look away from the sin we're about to commit," Johann murmured.

Loud cries from up ahead caught their attention. One of the horse-drawn carts shuddered and tipped. Four oil barrels slid off the back, falling to the ground and rolling wildly. They crashed into the trees along the path. One broke open, spilling the slick oil onto the mulch and grass. Edwin Roebling and Christian Hillenbrand ran after the other three.

Barend and Johann hurried up the hill. When they got to the tipped cart, Luther Möllhausen was already there, trying to calm the spooked horse. The same horse that had trampled his grandfather's crossbow, Barend noticed. "What happened?" he asked.

"The wheel came loose," Luther explained, and indeed Barend saw now that the front left wheel was tilted at an awkward angle under the weight of the cart.

Henry Maentel inspected the damage. "One of the bolts must have come free. It probably rolled into the woods there," he said, gesturing toward a spot where tall bushes grew alongside the trail.

Barend was certain the bolt must have loosened when the cart went over his crossbow. Feeling responsible, he went into the bushes first, pushing aside the small, prickly branches in his way. He scoured the ground for the missing bolt as the undergrowth scratched at his legs. Finally, on the other side of a thick curtain of shrubbery, he found a small clearing.

And froze in his tracks.

Four tall wooden spikes had been planted in the ground in the middle of the field. Impaled on them were four emaciated corpses, their limbs twisted, their jaws open in silent cries of agony, as if they were frozen in the process of dying. What little flesh was left after the birds had gotten to them was shriveled and stretched tight across their bones.

Barend's cry brought the others running. They burst through the bushes behind him and skidded to a halt.

"God protect us," Johann said, crossing himself over and over.

Henry and Edwin turned away, covering their mouths. Luther stared in wide-eyed horror.

Sunlight reflected off of something on one of the corpses, its gleam catching Barend's eye. "There's something there," he said. Though his nerves begged him not to get any closer, he moved in for a better look. The reflection flashed again, and he saw the metal links of a necklace half hidden in the tattered flesh of the corpse's neck. He followed the necklace with his eyes to a circular medallion lying against the exposed ribs. Saint Joseph.

"Oh, God," Barend said. "It's Christoph."

"The four Hellner brothers?" Edwin asked, appalled. "How? They've been dead two years, there shouldn't be anything left of them by now."

"He didn't kill them right away," Luther said grimly. "Look at their hands." Barend looked and immediately wished he hadn't. Some of the corpses' fingers were bent strangely, at right angles or all the way against the backs of their hands. Other fingers were missing entirely, leaving only ragged stubs protruding from the palm. The rest of their bodies had been mutilated, too—toes missing, genitals split in half, wounds in their torsos sutured numerous times, as if they'd been repeatedly cut open and sewn up. "He kept them alive," Luther said, his face clouding with anger and disgust. "As playthings."

By the time they found the bolt and fixed the wheel of the cart, Barend had nothing left in his stomach to vomit into the bushes. The sun was well across the sky when they started moving again. This time, he didn't stay in back with Johann. He joined Luther at the front. He didn't need the crossbow, not anymore. He didn't need anything but his bare hands to throttle the Necromancer until the light went out of the fiend's eyes.

The red, swollen sun was dipping toward the horizon when they reached the stone wall that surrounded Castle Karnstock. Locked wooden doors were embedded in the wall, and two great stone axes were perched atop the arch above them, their handles crossed to form an X, the age-old emblem of the House of Karnstock. The dying sun threw the shadow of those two great axes over them, and Barend shivered. The temperature within the shadow was unnaturally cold, and his hackles rose as though a thousand dead, freezing hands were reaching for him from just over his shoulder.

They used a thick battering ram to break the doors open, then poured through into the courtyard on other side. The castle loomed before them, an imposing silhouette against the twilight sky. All the windows were dark but one, high in a corner tower.

"What's wrong with the castle walls?" Edwin asked, pointing. "Look there. The stones are moving!"

"Those aren't stones," Luther said.

At that moment, innumerable tiny black eyes and sleek, ebony feathered heads turned in their direction. The castle was enveloped in blackbirds. They stood on windowsills, ledges, turrets, and parapets, so many that it was hard to tell what was stone and what was feather. They didn't make a sound, only blinked and cocked their heads, watching.

A shiver ran up Barend's spine, and for a moment he wished he'd stayed behind like Hahn Gehrig.

"He knows we're here," Henry Maentel whispered. "I can feel it."

"Good," Luther said. "Light up the torches. Let him see us coming. Let him know what it's like to be afraid."

The torches flared, reflected in a sea of blackbird eyes.

11.

The night after Edwin Roebling's body was found chopped to pieces in his kitchen, no one slept easy. It wasn't just the horror of the murder. There was something in the air, carried by the fog that had blanketed the village since sundown. It rolled through Helmburg, touching each home, and inside the villagers felt a foreboding in their bones. Something was coming.

Henry Maentel tossed restlessly. Beside him, his wife Carla groaned and turned away, pulling her pillow with her.

"Stop your fussing, Henry," she muttered. Then she was snoring again, and he continued staring at the ceiling.

He thought about Edwin's murder and the manure crosses on the Möllhausen house. Helmburg was falling out of his control. It was happening so quickly he couldn't figure out how or why, only that it was slipping through his fingers like water. In the five years since he'd become Bürgermeister, there'd been peace and prosperity. The only crimes to speak of were the rare drunken brawl at Huetten's Bierbrunnen or a candy-thieving child at the apothecary shop. That Helmburg seemed gone forever now. In its place was a dark, treacherous doppelgänger he didn't recognize.

He heard the front door open and his daughter Liese's footsteps on the stairs, coming home from her work at that blasted inn above Huetten's Bierbrunnen, no doubt. He'd made it clear he didn't approve, but his displeasure meant nothing to her. She was young and headstrong, she didn't understand about status and station. Henry sighed. It wasn't just the village he was losing control of. It was his daughter, too.

It was worse now that Kasch was back. Liese never talked to Henry about such things, but he knew there was something between those two. Fathers always knew, even if they didn't let on. His daughter had cried for days after Luther sent Kasch away, and refused to come out of her room. Now the boy was back in Helmburg and asking too many questions. That wasn't good. Yet if he ordered his daughter to stay away from him, she wouldn't obey him any more than she had about working at the inn.

He closed his eyes. The darkness behind his eyelids dipped and swirled, took on shape and color, and then he was standing in the woods. Four tall wooden spikes stood before him. Impaled on one of them was the corpse of Edwin Roebling. The other three were bare. Waiting.

Hahn Gehrig dreamed fitfully of Black Easter. He'd stayed home that day and watched from the window of his second-story flat as Luther Möllhausen led his small army to the castle. He'd shaken his head and called them fools as the villagers closed the gates behind them. But in his dream he was with them, entering the castle with Edwin Roebling at his side. Dark shapes flew at them out of the shadows, ink-black wings flapping just over their heads. Hahn ducked behind Edwin. When they'd passed, he straightened again and searched the roof beams.

"Are there more of them?" he demanded, his voice wavering. "Are we safe now?"

"Everyone knows why you stayed home," Edwin said. "Everyone knows you're a coward. Even you."

When he turned, Edwin was gone. There was only a sheet bundled on the floor, dark red pools seeping through the white linen.

Kasch lay in bed and thought maybe the crazy old priest was right. He shouldn't have come back. There was nothing for him here. He liked Hahn well enough, but the old man was no reason to stay. Neither was Liese, he thought with a hollowness in his chest, not if she believed such awful things about him.

There was a bank in Bern he used to walk by all the time, a sign in its window offering to buy property at a fair price, sight-unseen. He could sell the house and land, and make enough money to start a new life somewhere else. Cut all ties with Helmburg for good.

He'd go tomorrow, he decided. He wouldn't even say goodbye. Why bother? No one would miss him anyway.

He closed his eyes and felt himself drift into sleep. And then she was there, the woman he'd dreamed of before, emerging from the infinite dark. She pushed her honey-colored hair back from her face, her almond-shaped eyes twinkling at him.

"You don't really want to leave, do you?" she whispered. "If you leave, we can't be together."

He stared at the small birthmark beside her mouth and burned with desire for her. With the confidence that comes with dreaming, he reached for her to pull her close, but she slipped out of his grasp.

"Stay," she said. "Stay because no one else will love you like I do."

Johann Vierick slept in an empty stall of a private stable, on a bed of straw that smelled of horse urine. The stable provided a warm place to sleep, and so far he'd been lucky to find it unlocked every night. Its owner hadn't discovered him yet, nor had any of the people who rented the flats above it, and for that he was grateful. If they forced him from the stable, he doubted he would ever find another place as comfortable.

But tonight there was no comfort. Since sundown he'd been having feverish half-dreams of an eyeless Savior crucified beneath the peaked roof of a wooden hutch. He rolled onto his stomach, and something hard and sharp poked his chest, waking him. He turned onto his back and revealed the culprit—the silver cross that hung from his neck. He held it up to look at it. There was a smudge on one of its arms, a fingerprint or some dirt. He licked his thumb, ignoring the taste of weeks' worth of grime and dusty earth, and tried to rub the smudge away.

He had to keep the cross shiny and clean. This way the voices would never forget that it was there to protect him. Because without the cross, the voices would take form, they would develop hideous, terrifying bodies and come to tear him apart with their claws.

He noticed the fresh cuts on his hands, and remembered slipping and putting his hand through one of the windows at the Möllhausen house. Why had he gone there? A pinpoint of light reflected off the silver cross into his eye. Yes, he remembered now, the crosses. Crosses were protection. Crosses repelled evil.

His mind stumbled and tripped through time, showing him memories he'd rather forget. He saw whispering shadows that crawled on the walls, pale hands that reached up for him out of a dark pit. Past, present, and future merged, melted, and reformed as a big silver cross.

He kept rubbing at the smudge, his breath growing labored. In the next stall, a chocolate-brown mare eyed him over the low wall and blew air out of her nose disdainfully.

"It takes a lot of work to keep it polished," he explained to the horse. "Sometimes I find blood on it."

In his modest flat above the same stable, Barend Lang wasn't sleeping at all. He couldn't stop thinking about Johann. The old priest was probably already asleep downstairs in the stable—every night, Barend made sure to leave its doors unlocked so Johann had a safe place to sleep—but he couldn't bring himself to go down there and arrest him. Not after all they'd been through.

It was obvious Johann's madness had escalated. Vandalizing Kasch's house was proof of that. But murder? Was he capable of such a thing? And why Edwin, of all people? They'd been friends. They'd fought side by side on Black Easter. All of them had.

Barend rolled over in bed, and something caught his eye in the corner of the bedroom. He raised himself on an elbow. It was too dark to see anything but a vague silhouette against the wall. His skin prickled, and his body tensed with adrenaline. Someone was in the room with him.

"Who's there?" His voice cracked, sounding weak and frightened to his own ears. There was no answer from the dark corner, only the sound of breathing.

He fumbled to light a match from the box on the bedside table. It flared, illuminating the bedroom in a warm orange glow.

Rebekah stood in the corner, but not as he remembered her from the day she disappeared. During their picnic in the Rosenmann fields, she'd been vibrant, apple-cheeked, her skin pink and glowing. The thing in the corner with his fiancée's face had skin as white as paper, corroded slabs of metal bolted to her flesh, and a mouth sewn shut with thick strands of wire.

The match burned his fingertips. He dropped it, and it snuffed out on the floor. With trembling hands, he grabbed another and lit it. The match flared, lighting the room again. The corner was empty.

Had he really seen Rebekah? No, that abomination couldn't be her. Telling Kasch about losing her to the Necromancer had brought up bad memories, played tricks on his mind, that was all.

Still, he had to be sure. He took the lantern from its hook on the wall and lit it. Holding it aloft, he inspected the entire bedroom. When the lantern's light fell on the bedroom door, he saw the long bronze handle depress. Someone was on the other side, trying to get in. He stalked over, grabbed the handle, and yanked the door open. Rebekah stood in the hallway—not the monstrosity he'd seen in the corner, but the healthy nineteen-year-old girl he'd been betrothed to so many years ago, wearing the same robin's-egg-blue sundress she'd worn the last time he saw her.

She opened her arms to him, smiled, and said, "Barend, my love."

He backed away and almost dropped the lantern.

Rebekah stepped over the threshold and into the bedroom. "I've missed you so much," she said.

He shook his head. Her voice, God, her voice, hearing it again soothed the wound he thought would never heal. He wanted to embrace her, spin her around in his arms like when they were young, and yet...

She frowned, pouting her ruby lips in a way that Barend could never resist. "Why are you looking at me like that?" she asked. "Don't you want to know what he did to me? Up in that cold, dark castle all alone?"

"No," he said. "This isn't real. This is a dream."

"You always loved puzzles, Barend. Figuring things out. Don't you want to know why he took me, why he took all of us?"

He squeezed his eyes shut and clenched his fists. "Wake up, Barend, you old fool."

"Kiss me," she said. "Kiss me like you used to, like you would have on our wedding night."

The thought of kissing his lost love one more time threatened to break his heart in two. He opened his eyes and saw a wire sewn through her lips. Pieces of metal bolted to her skin. "You're not real!" he cried.

He retreated until the backs of his legs hit the bed. The lantern fell from his hand, its base striking the floor with a metallic clang. The flame flickered, and the horrible half-metal creature was gone. There was only Rebekah in her pretty blue dress. She put her arms around him. He closed his watering eyes, praying he'd wake up soon. If it wasn't real, he couldn't bear any more of it.

She was soft and warm, and he could feel her breath on his neck when she said, "What's the matter, my love? Don't you want me anymore? Don't you know me?" She pulled away, and when he opened his eyes again, she was gone. Everything had turned misty, a gray fog filling the room. It was so thick he couldn't see more than a few inches in front of him.

She was gone. She'd come back to him, a miracle, and like a fool he'd turned her away.

"Rebekah?" he called. "Where are you?" His lip trembled. The yearning inside him was so strong he thought he would explode. "Please don't leave me again," he whispered to the mist.

Something moved, a shape in the distance. As it grew closer, he saw a figure coming toward him.

"Rebekah?" Tears of relief rolled down his cheek. "I'm sorry. Please stay. Please, I need you."

The figure came closer. It was taller than Rebekah, he noticed suddenly, and its shape was not that of a woman. Something shiny and silver reflected the lantern's light back to him. He'd seen this before, a reflection in the fog, but it took him a moment to remember where. The alley near the tavern. The glint of lamplight off a big silver cross.

"Johann?" Barend asked, confused.

The figure rushed at him, swinging something that struck him hard and sharp in the chest.

12.

When Johann opened his eyes the next morning, he discovered he was lying on the stone steps of the church. He smiled faintly. The church called him back each night without fail, called him out of the stable and held his sleeping body to its bosom. It kept him safe. One day the church would shake off the nailed wooden boards and open its doors to him again. Then everything would be back to the way it was. Everything would be right again.

He sat up and winced. The voices were loud today, like hundreds of mouths hissing right next to his ear. He looked up, trying to spot the ruined castle on the mountainside, but the clouds hung too low, a gray roof over Helmburg. He laughed and jumped up triumphantly.

"You can't see me!" he shouted into the distance. "I don't care what you say, you can't see me, you can't make me do anything! You might as well stop trying!" The whispering grew louder, more insistent, a multitude of voices speaking at once, all of them demanding something of him. Johann cradled his head again. "Stop it! I won't listen!"

But there was something else too this time, something behind the voices. A tolling bell. He looked up at the church, but its bell remained a motionless shadow within the slatted windows of the belfry. Nonetheless, the tolling continued. *The castle*, he thought. It had to be coming from the castle.

He covered his ears. They were only trying to scare him. They were dead, they couldn't do anything to him, only whisper and make phantom bell sounds.

Keeping his hands over his ears, he stepped down off the church stairs and started walking. Villagers rushed past him, running and

shouting, shoving him out of the way in their haste. He didn't turn to see where they were headed. It didn't matter. The whole village—
—*will drown in blood.*

"Stop it," Johann said. "You don't scare me anymore. Do you hear? You're just voices. I don't have to listen to you—"
—*scream, listen to you scream, listen to you scream.*

More people hurried past, almost knocking him to the ground. He scurried to the side of the street to get out of their way, and stood by the tavern door. Something bad was happening, and the bell was still tolling, he heard it through his hands. He didn't want to take his hands away from his ears. It wasn't safe to, not yet. Not until the voices quieted down, then he could put—
—*you in the pit, put you in the pit, in the pit with the others.*

He squeezed his eyes shut. He couldn't take much more. The voices were—
—*coming back, we're coming back, coming.*
For you.
For all of you.

He opened his eyes again and saw a short, balding man cross the street angrily toward him. Behind him were six more men, each much bigger than the bald one. They had the grimy look of blacksmiths. He knew these men from somewhere, and tried to piece together the flashes of recognition that seeped through the noise in his head.

Then the short, bald one was yelling at him, but he couldn't hear because his hands were still over his ears. Behind the yelling man—Fritz, that was his name, Fritz Gruber, he owned both the metalworking shops in Helmburg—behind him the big men, his blacksmiths, cracked their knuckles and glared. Finally, Fritz grabbed Johann's wrists and pulled his hands away from his ears. Suddenly, the tolling was louder. It wasn't coming from the castle after all, he realized. It was the alarm bell in front of the constabulary.

"You may have the rest of them fooled, but not us!" Fritz shouted. "You couldn't resist chopping up another one, could you, *priest*?" He spat the last word scornfully. "Did the voices in your head tell you to kill Barend, too?"

"Barend is dead?" Johann asked, confused. First Edwin, and now Barend? A thought came to him, vague and smoky, trying to squeeze through the knots in his mind. Everything came in patterns. The murders had a pattern, too.

Fritz grabbed him by the neck and pushed him against the wall. "Why'd you do it?" He squeezed Johann's neck, throttling him.

"No use asking a crazy man why," one of the blacksmiths said. "Let's just get this over with. Mad dogs need to be put down."

"They should have locked up this goddamn lunatic years ago," Fritz snarled.

Johann coughed and choked. *A pattern*, he wanted to say, but the voices whispered loudly in his ear until all he could do was release their words through his mouth. "Village," he croaked. "Drown...in blood..."

Fritz's eyes widened and he let go of Johann's neck. "What did you say? Was that a threat?"

"He's a goddamn menace, this one," another blacksmith said. "Let's teach him a lesson in civility."

The blacksmith slammed his meaty fist into Johann's stomach. He dropped onto the cobblestones, coughing and spitting. The men surrounded him, kicking their heavy boots into his ribs, back, and stomach. Each blow sent shockwaves of pain through him. Fists struck the back of his head, knocking his face into the cobblestones, and he tasted blood. He crawled, scraping himself across the hard stones, trying to get away. "Where do you think you're going?" one of them said. He couldn't tell which one. Fritz and his men were a single creature now, speaking in unison with their fists and feet. A boot connected with his spine, and colored lights flashed behind his eyelids. The voices from the castle laughed and laughed.

The blows ceased then, and Johann opened his eyes tentatively. The men were still there, standing in a circle around him. Fritz reached down, grabbed a handful of Johann's hair, and pulled him up onto his knees. Then he reached into his belt with his free hand and pulled out a long hunting knife.

"Lesson's over," Fritz said. "It's time to put an end to this."

He yanked Johann's head back, pulling the skin taut on his exposed neck. He held the knife to Johann's throat.

"Wait," Johann croaked, drooling blood. The cold metal of the blade against his skin made his arms twitch in panic. Fritz pulled his hair tighter to get him under control.

"There'll be no more murders in Helmburg," Fritz said.

"You have to listen to me," Johann said. "It's not over. It's the castle! It's alive, it's—it's just sleeping, and when it wakes up *everyone* will die!"

"Did he just threaten us again?" one of the blacksmiths said. He shook his head. "Some lessons just don't take."

Fritz drew his knife arm back, preparing to slash Johann's throat. Johann shut his eyes and thought, *yes, finally, just let it end*, but the blade never came. He opened one eye to peek at Fritz. The bald little man was staring at something. Johann turned to see what it was, and gasped. There, watching them from where it stood on the cobblestones, was the biggest blackbird he'd ever seen. Thick and fat, it let out a sharp caw, and another caw answered from nearby. Johann looked across the street at the cracked sign hanging in front of the apothecary shop. A second blackbird was perched atop it, the sign swinging ominously under its weight.

A shadow fell over them then. At first, Johann thought an enormous cloud must have passed in front of the sun, but then he looked up. Hundreds of blackbirds flew against the gray backdrop of the sky, so many of them that they merged into a single amorphous black shape, a living canopy, a screeching storm cloud. They circled, wheeled, and plunged down toward the village.

"Holy God," Fritz whispered. The knife slipped from his hand. He let go of Johann's hair and stepped out into the street. The blackbirds were suddenly everywhere, swooping, pecking, and clawing, so many that they looked to Johann like black holes torn in the fabric of reality. Windows shattered. Screams rang out as villagers scrambled to get out of the street.

Fritz and his blacksmiths ran, disappearing into the chaos. Johann threw himself flat on the street to avoid the swooping claws and beaks. In front of him was Fritz's dropped hunting knife. He picked it up, held it tight, and didn't let go.

13.

Kasch was riding through Helmburg in a hired coach, heading for the gates and the world outside, when the tolling of the bell began. He remembered what Hahn had told him, how the bell meant there was an emergency somewhere in the village. What was it this time? No doubt Inspector Barend Lang was rushing to Kasch's house right now with more questions and smug insinuations about this latest crisis. Too bad for the Inspector that Kasch wouldn't be there to hear them.

As the coach trundled over the cobblestones, he remembered what the beautiful woman in his dream had told him, that they couldn't be together if he left. He felt a momentary sting of regret, then chuckled at his own foolishness. She was a figment of his lonely imagination, not a real woman. What was to stop him from dreaming of her at an inn in Prague or a flat in Stuttgart?

The coachman, a skinny man with a tall stovepipe hat and scruffy muttonchops, leaned off his perch and called back to Kasch, "The alarm bell! Do you want to stop?"

"Keep going," he replied through the window.

"Just like yesterday," the coachman continued. "Terrible. Do you think it's another one done in like that Roebling fellow?"

Kasch didn't answer. He knew the coachman was eager for conversation to calm his nerves, but he only wanted to get to Bern, sell his property to the bank and be done with it. He hadn't even wasted time packing his clothes. He'd buy a whole new wardrobe with the money from the sale.

He looked at his injured hand. The handkerchief had come undone in the night, lost somewhere in the bed, and the scabs had broken open again. Fresh blood trickled along his knuckles. He licked the thumb of his other hand and used it to wipe away the blood.

As the coach turned onto the main thoroughfare, Kasch glanced out the window. A crowd of villagers ran past, responding to the alarm bell. They moved in a great pack, like animals, and bumped into the coach in their haste. The horse in front whinnied, and the coach shook alarmingly, then stopped altogether. Kasch leaned out the window to see what was happening. The horse reared, hoofing at the air and snorting.

The coachman pulled the reins, trying to bring the horse under control. "It's the crowd, sir!" he shouted. "They're spooking him!"

The horse dropped down again and shook his head spastically, tossing his mane and making noises Kasch had never heard from a horse before. Something wasn't right, he thought. It wasn't just the crowd that had spooked the horse.

The horse bucked and kicked back at the coach. He broke the wooden beams on either side and snapped his tethers. The coach tipped forward, throwing Kasch against the cushioned seat opposite him as the horse galloped away, whinnying insanely, and disappeared down a side street. Groaning, Kasch picked himself up and opened the door, stepping onto the cobblestone street. The coachman was already down from his perch and checking the damage. The front of the coach had been kicked to pieces, but the coachman was unharmed, save for his crumpled stovepipe hat.

"I'm sorry," the coachman said. "I don't know what happened. He's never acted like that before, and he's seen his share of crowds, believe me."

"What about the coach?" Kasch asked

The coachman shook his head and took off his hat. "She isn't going anywhere until she's fixed, and that'll be at least a day."

Kasch watched the crowd streaming past. "We'll take another of your coaches, then."

"I'm afraid not. She's the only one I've got until my partner brings the other back from Köln."

"Christ," Kasch groaned, covering his face.

"I can take you tomorrow," the coachman said. "That's the best I can offer."

Kasch sighed. Another day in Helmburg would feel like an

unbearable eternity. He had to leave now. "Curse it, I'll walk if I have to," he said.

The coachman squinted at him. "All the way to Bern?"

Kasch didn't answer him. He dropped a handful of coins into the coachman's hand and started walking toward the gates. He only got a few yards before another wave of villagers came running out of the side streets to see what the emergency was. He tried to wind his way through them, but it was like swimming against an overpowering current. Elbows, knees, and shoulders jarred him, spun him around. He felt lightheaded, and was sure he suddenly smelled ash somewhere nearby. He couldn't breathe. His vision darkened as he pushed his way through the jostling crowd. Another blackout was coming on, he was sure of it. He fought against it, struggling not to give in, and shouted at the people to move aside. But they didn't, they were a mindless swarm, the bees of Helmburg, and somewhere their invisible queen had commanded them to stop him from reaching the gates. Helmburg wasn't going to let him leave.

Up ahead, he saw Johann wading through the crowd toward the tavern across the street. Kasch steered clear. The last thing he needed was more trouble from Helmburg's resident madman. Kasch kept pushing forward against the tide until the crowd thinned, died away, and then he was standing before the open gates. The creeping blackness faded from his vision, and the smell of ash dissipated. He breathed deeply, calming himself, regaining control.

Beyond the gates was the dirt road that led up to the mountain pass. If he was lucky, he might be able to hitch a ride with a passing coach, or hire a new one in the next village. Either way, Helmburg would be at his back for good.

He stepped through the gates and onto the road. Then he laughed. He'd won. Helmburg had tried to stop him, but it had failed. There was nothing it could do now to keep him there.

A piercing cry cut the air above him, and he glanced up. Blackbirds, more than he could count, obscured the sky, flying down from the mountains and into the valley. Into the village. They swooped like a tidal wave, a wall of feathers and claws coming right for him. Kasch dropped to the ground. The birds passed over him, screeching and cawing. He was back on his feet an instant later and saw more blackbirds winging toward him. He turned and sprinted away from them in the only direction he could—back through the gates into Helmburg. Villagers ran in confusion and terror, covering their heads and swatting at the diving black shapes. The high-pitched cacophony of bird cries and human screams felt like nails being driven into his ears.

Liese ran out of the pandemonium and toward the tavern. Two birds flew behind her, Kasch saw, snapping at loose strands of her hair. He started toward her, pushing his way through the panicked crowd, trying not to lose sight of her. Liese tried the tavern door, but it didn't open. She shouted and banged on it. A wing grazed Kasch's hair, and he ducked, losing sight of her. Someone collided with him then, and he spun, twisting his ankle painfully. When he straightened again, he saw Liese had pressed herself against the tavern wall, protected from above by the building's eaves.

Someone else was with her. Johann. The old priest held a big hunting knife in his hand. His face was covered with blood. *God, no*, Kasch thought, and ran toward the tavern, cursing his twisted ankle for slowing him down. "Liese!" he yelled.

She spotted, the terror on her face briefly turning to relief. "Kasch, what's happening?"

"Liese, get away from him!"

Johann turned, the blade in his hand glinting.

When Kasch reached the tavern, he grabbed Liese's hand and pulled her as far from Johann as he could.

"What's happening?" she repeated, her voice high and full of panic. He wrapped his arms around her, and she buried her head in his chest.

Kasch glared over her head at Johann. "Stay away."

"It isn't over," the old priest said, shaking his head. Blood dripped from his mouth. He wiped it away. "They should have listened to me. Now it's too late. He's here. He's come back for the rest of us."

A man ran by suddenly, a blackbird gripping his collar in its claws and flapping its wings spastically. It pecked at the man's cheek and ear. His neck and shoulder were slick with blood. Liese screamed and turned away.

"But the hour cometh, and now is," Johann continued. "Mark my words. This village will drown in blood, just as he said it would."

Johann tucked the knife into his belt, clutched tight the big silver cross around his neck, and walked out into the street. Kasch winced, expecting the birds to attack the old priest immediately, but they parted to let him pass unharmed, like Moses through the Red Sea. Kasch watched, dumbfounded, as the birds ignored Johann until he disappeared from sight.

"Did you see that?" he whispered. "They—they let him go."

Liese looked up at him, her eyes wide and rimmed with red. "Why is this happening?"

"I don't know," Kasch said. "Are you all right?"

She nodded. "I was at the cemetery, visiting my brother Abelard's grave. I try to go there once a week to watch the sunrise with him. It's foolish, I know the grave is empty, but it still feels like he's there with me. Then there was that awful bell, and the blackbirds..." She cringed and shook her head. "What did we do to deserve this?"

"Kasch!" someone called. He turned and spotted Hahn standing under the eaves of the building across the street. The old man motioned for them to cross the thoroughfare to him.

"Is he mad?" Liese demanded. She looked up at the bird-filled sky. "I'm not going anywhere."

"My flat!" Hahn shouted, pointing frantically back in the direction of the gates. "It's safer than being out in the open!"

Behind them, the loud crash of shattering glass startled Kasch. He and Liese spun and saw blackbirds swarming into the empty tavern through a broken window in the opposite wall.

"We can't stay here," he said, but Liese still looked too frightened by the idea of leaving their protected spot. He couldn't blame her. The blackbirds might have spared Johann, but clearly everyone else was fair game. "Hold onto me and keep your head down. No matter what happens, just keep moving, all right?"

She nodded, digging her nails into him through his shirt, and together they launched themselves into the street. Kasch couldn't see where he was going with all the black shapes speeding by his face. He felt the hard slap of wings against his head, and the graze of talons swooping past him.

"Come on!" Hahn shouted, holding his arms out toward them. A blackbird dove past him, and he cringed, yanking his arms back quickly.

Kasch gripped Liese tighter to pull her along, then realized he wasn't pulling her, it was the other way around. His twisted ankle was slowing him down, and she was leading him across the thoroughfare.

She screamed as a blackbird tangled its claws in her hair. It flapped and squawked, and Kasch swatted at it until it flew off.

"I'm too slow," he told her. "Let go of me and run."

Liese didn't say anything. She kept her head low and continued pulling him across the thoroughfare.

"That's it, keep going!" Hahn cried. He reached out for them again. Kasch grabbed one of Hahn's hands, Liese the other, and Hahn pulled them to the wall beside him. The old man laughed with relief. "Come on, follow me. My flat isn't far." Hugging the wall, he started moving away with Liese right behind him.

Kasch stayed a moment, watching the bedlam around them. There were fewer people on the street now, but the skies, roofs, and gables were alive with blackbirds. A dead man lay in the gutter. The birds had shredded his clothes, leaving his white waistcoat stained with blood. There was a wet, red hole in his face where his eye should have been.

Something flashed brightly on the cobblestones in the distance, catching his attention. It came from near the broken-down coach he'd tried to take out of Helmburg, in the spot where the horse had spooked. At first he thought he was looking at just another cobblestone, but it couldn't be. Cobblestones weren't white, and they certainly didn't glow from within like a lamp. It had to be a reflection in a puddle or a piece of glass, but still, he could almost hear it buzzing in his head. No, not buzzing. Calling. Pulling him. It reminded him of how he felt when the blackouts came, in those last floating moments before losing consciousness.

"Come on, Kasch!" Hahn shouted, grabbing him and pulling him away.

14.

Up in his second-story flat, Hahn peered nervously out the living room window. "They're still out there," he said. His hands trembled as he wiped the sweat from his brow.

Next to him, Kasch shook his head in disbelief. He couldn't see the cobblestones on the street below for all the blackbirds. They were a conquering force, and the town was theirs now. "I've never seen anything like this," he said.

"I have," Hahn said. "Once, years ago, on Black Easter. The sky was filled with them that night. They passed over the village, going God-knows-where, but they didn't come down. They didn't do *this*."

"It's why you're supposed to kill a blackbird when you see it," Liese said. She was sitting on the couch behind them, her legs tucked up under her. She'd refused to go near the window. "That's what they say, isn't it? You're supposed to kill it or it'll bring bad luck. We must have killed hundreds over the years, and now they've come for revenge."

"You don't honestly believe that, do you?" Kasch asked.

Liese chewed a fingernail. "I don't know."

"If I had a rifle, I'd kill each and every one of them," Hahn said. "Or silver. Silver is supposed to work against the dark forces."

"They're just birds," Kasch said. "Something must have set them off."

Hahn laughed bitterly. "Just birds, he says. You're more naive than I thought, boy. Open your eyes. This isn't some random catastrophe. This is an omen. A sign. I knew this would happen. I *told* them it would. We thought we were safe, but then Edwin and Barend were murdered. I should have put the pieces together sooner."

"Wait," Kasch said. "Barend is dead?"

Hahn nodded. "It happened last night. He was hacked to pieces, just like Edwin."

Kasch's legs felt weak, and he sat down in the chair at Hahn's writing desk. The Inspector was dead. That explained why the alarm bell had tolled all morning. He turned to the desk and saw there wasn't much on it but a quill pen, a bottle of ink, and a single piece of paper held down by a glass paperweight. Wrinkled and yellowed, the paper looked like it had been there for ages. It was blank except for the words *My Dearest Jenelle* written across the top.

"Don't you see?" Hahn said, pulling Kasch's attention back to him. "It's the Necromancer. He's come back!"

"But Kasch's father killed him," Liese said. "Everyone knows that."

"Tosh! What does death mean to someone who wields power over the dead?" Hahn insisted. "There were five survivors of Black Easter. Edwin and Barend were two of them, and now they're dead. Murdered the same way. It's that monster's revenge, I know it. They never should have gone to the castle that day."

Liese shook her head. "You're mad. Are you really saying the Necromancer's ghost killed those men?"

Hahn nodded. "Yes, yes I am. It was him, or someone under his control."

Kasch rolled his eyes in frustration, but at the same time he couldn't deny that strange things were happening in Helmburg. *Someone* had killed Edwin and Barend. He didn't believe in the supernatural, only that Hahn's own superstition and fear were preventing the old man from seeing that a killer was in their midst. A killer who knew both victims well enough to sneak in and out of their homes without detection, and who was unhinged enough to commit murders this savage. Maybe even insane enough to not remember doing it. To him, there was only one logical suspect. "The priest," he said.

Hahn stopped pacing and turned to him. "Johann?"

"His mind is gone," Kasch said. "He claims the castle talks to him, and he's been getting more agitated recently, more unpredictable and violent." He'd also walked through the blackbirds unharmed, Kasch thought. He wasn't sure what it meant, but he couldn't stop thinking about it.

Hahn shook his head. "No, not Johann. That's impossible. He's a man of God."

"Not anymore," Kasch said.

"He wouldn't hurt a fly," Hahn insisted angrily. "You don't know him."

"I'm sure you've already heard what he did to my house. Is that something a sane man would do?"

Hahn frowned. "Crosses made of horse manure. Why would Johann do that?"

"Because he's insane," Kasch said. "Face it, Hahn, you don't know what he's capable of. The man you remember doesn't exist anymore."

Hahn shook his head. "No, it can't be Johann. It doesn't sit right."

"Who then?" Kasch pressed. "Who else could it be?"

"There's another explanation," Hahn said, "but it's too terrible."

Kasch almost laughed. "Hahn, the village was just attacked by blackbirds. I think we're past the point of judging what's too terrible to consider."

The old man nodded. "True enough. It's just...I was thinking, what if your father didn't kill the Necromancer? What if he only thought he did? Or worse, only *said* he did?"

"Now I know you're mad," Liese said. "It's been twenty years since Black Easter. If Luther didn't kill him, what's the Necromancer been doing all this time? Sewing?"

"Planning his revenge," Hahn said. "Gathering his strength. Waiting for the right time."

The sudden din of fluttering wings made them jump. The window turned black as a massive wave of birds took off into the sky, the conquering army abandoning its spoils. Kasch looked down at the empty street. Dark rivulets of blood gathered around the cobblestones below.

"They're gone!" Liese said.

"Yes, but for how long, that's the question," Hahn said. He pressed his face against the glass and searched the sky.

"Do you think it's safe to go outside?" Liese asked.

"I would wait," Hahn said. "They may not have gone far."

"I can't stay, I have to make sure my parents are all right," Liese said. "Kasch, will you walk with me?"

He nodded, then turned to Hahn. "I'd like to come back tomorrow, if that's all right with you. I have a lot of questions, and I think you can help me."

"Questions about what?" the old man asked.

"My father, for one. There were things that happened before I was born, and things that happened after I left."

Hahn waved a hand dismissively. "You know everything there is to know."

"Please, Hahn, I need your help. You're one of the few people in Helmburg I trust."

Hahn sat down on the couch with a heavy sigh, and ran his hands over his face. "Ah, boy, never get old," he said. "It's not just your aging bones that wear you out, it's the burden on your soul, too. You hear things and then wish you could forget them." He shook his head again. "Old men are supposed to lose their memories, not relive what's dead and gone."

Kasch looked at Liese in confusion. She shrugged back at him.

"Hahn," he said loudly, trying to snap the old man out of his reverie. "I'll be back tomorrow. I want you to tell me everything about my parents."

"Ha!" The old man looked heavenward. "Now he wants to know about *both* of them! Sweet old papa and loving mama." He stood up. "I may be old, boy, but I'm no fool. There are some things you don't want to know, and you'll blame me for telling you."

Kasch blinked. Liese turned to him, widening her eyes and tilting her head toward the door, signaling it was time to leave.

"Tomorrow," Kasch repeated. "I need to know, Hahn."

"Fine, so be it," Hahn snapped. "But if you don't like what you hear," he slapped his palms together, "I wash my hands of it."

Outside, Liese hooked her arm through his as they wound their way around the constables collecting the bodies of the dead, and around the pools of blood and black feathers on the street. They stayed on the side of the street, and doors opened as they passed and villagers poked their heads out to check the skies.

"I don't think you should go back there tomorrow," Liese said. "In fact, I don't think you should spend any more time with Hahn at all. I don't think he's a safe person to know."

"He's nice enough, normally," Kasch said.

"Then he's got you fooled," she said. "There's nothing nice about that man. He's mad."

"He's the only friend I've got."

She turned to face him. "How can you say that? You've got me, haven't you? I'm your friend."

"Are you?" he asked.

Her mouth dropped open in offense. "What do you mean by that? Of course I am!"

"I heard what your friend said at the tavern last night, Liese, the red-haired woman," Kasch said. "She said some terrible things about me."

"Erika?" Liese laughed. "She's a gossip who's always looking for scandals to keep herself entertained. Don't pay her any attention. She didn't grow up with you. She doesn't know you the way I do."

Kasch stopped walking. "I don't care what *she* thinks, Liese. I care what *you* think, and you agreed with her."

"Kasch, I only agreed with her to make her stop. You don't know Erika. That's the only way to get her to shut up."

"So you don't think I'm trouble?" he asked.

"Oh, I didn't say that," she said with a sly grin. "I just don't think you're the *bad* kind of trouble."

Their eyes met, and Kasch remembered standing with her in the cellar of Huetten's Bierbrunnen, only thirteen years old but feeling eternal because he was in love. He remembered how they'd kissed, tentatively at first, unsure if they were doing it right, and then broke apart and laughed and tried again until the barkeep found them and chased them out.

Liese started walking again. "Remember when we used to float paper boats down the stream behind your house?" she asked. "Those are my favorite memories. Everything was so much easier when we were children. We didn't have a care in the world except how far we could make those boats sail. I wish life was always like that. I wish we could go back and stay that way."

"So do I," Kasch said. "Just go back and start over. Only this time I'd do things differently. I wouldn't let my father send me away, and I wouldn't wait as long as I did..." He trailed off, glancing at her. "Things would be different, that's all."

She looked up at him. "Come see me tomorrow instead of that crazy old man. Promise you will."

"I'd like that," he said, and reached for her hand.

A shrill, high-pitched note speared his ears suddenly, so loud he thought it would mince his brain. He clasped his hands over his ears but couldn't block it out.

Liese gaped at him. "Kasch? Are you all right?"

The noise stabbed painfully into his brain, and he dropped to his knees with a cry.

"Kasch!" He could barely hear Liese's cry over the sound.

He clamped his eyes shut and pushed his hands harder against his ears, but nothing helped. He tipped forward, collapsing onto the street.

"Kasch, what is it? What's wrong?"

The noise intensified, growing louder until he thought his eardrums would rupture. He opened his eyes and saw charcoal-gray cobblestones in front of his face. No, they weren't all gray. One was so starkly white it looked as if it had been painted. But the color wasn't artificial, he knew that the moment he saw it. The pallor came from inside it somehow.

So did the noise tearing through his head.

Gritting his teeth, praying his skull wouldn't split in two, he reached for the white cobblestone.

"Kasch, answer me!" Liese yelled from the end of a long tunnel.

His fingers touched the stone's hard surface.

At last.

As soon as he heard the strange voice in his head, images exploded behind his eyes, so abrupt and distorted he couldn't be sure what he was seeing. A struggling young man chained to a dark stone wall, his lips stitched together with wire, his body convulsing and twisting until the skin of his side swelled and ruptured, and something as white and thick as paste burst out of the wound.

Don't you know me?

The images jumped and shattered. He saw jagged shards of metal welded to sickly pale flesh, eyes rolled back with the whites pierced by metal nails. Mutilated, disfigured shapes lumbered toward him. Hands reached for him out of the darkness. Dead hands.

I know you.
Kasch.

Kasch pulled his hand off the white cobblestone. As soon as he did, the noise and visions stopped.

"Help! Someone help us!" Liese shouted.

Kasch rolled onto his back and saw her looking down at him, terrified. Other faces appeared as villagers gathered around. Blackness crept into the corners of his vision, the smell of ash hit his nose, and he felt himself slipping away.

God, no, please, he thought, *not now, not in front of them, not in front of* her. He felt hands grabbing him, but he couldn't tell if they were lifting him up off the ground or pulling him down through the cobblestones. Then the world turned black and disappeared.

15.

BLACK EASTER, 1826

Two crossed axes, similar to those that stood above the entrance to the courtyard, had been carved into the wooden double doors of Castle Karnstock, made to look as if they were crossing over the seam. Standing in the back of the group, Father Johann Vierick watched Luther Möllhausen, Barend Lang, and Edwin Roebling smash the doors open with the battering ram.

Luther divided the men into two groups, ten to go inside and five to remain outside to pile the hay, twigs, and barrels of oil from the carts around the perimeter of the castle, and then wait for his word. Johann could see the apprehension in those five men's eyes at the thought of waiting out in the open. They wanted to set torch to the kindling now and run back to the village. He couldn't blame them, not with the blackbirds perched on the walls and battlements staring down at them like that. The emptiness of their eyes made cold sweat pool at the small of his back.

"Father, you're with us," Luther said, motioning him forward. Johann joined him, and as they moved toward the door, he clutched his Bible with one hand and grasped the silver cross hanging around his neck with the other. In front of him, Henry Maentel cracked open his double-barreled rifle and slid two bullets from his pocket into the chambers, then crossed the threshold into the castle. Johann followed, wishing he had a rifle, too. The dagger hidden in his boot felt small and useless all of a sudden.

Inside, a massive hall extended into the darkness, its walls soaring upward to an arched ceiling some thirty feet above them, the first stars of evening now visible through the high, vaulted windows. The men moved forward slowly, their footsteps echoing off the stone walls. It made the castle sound empty, Johann thought. As lifeless as a tomb.

Two parallel rows of marble statues formed a corridor that led down the center of the hall—twisted, nightmarish things with gaping mouths, crooked limbs, and smooth planes of stone where their eyes should be. Whoever had carved these grotesqueries must have been mad.

Johann was already on edge when a hint of movement by the wall caught his eye. He turned toward it quickly. Out of reach of the torches, the shadows shrouding the wall seemed infinite, impenetrable. He tapped Barend's shoulder in front of him, and said, "Over there. Give it some light."

Barend swung his torch around. There was nothing there, just a simple wall, and yet Johann could have sworn he saw the shadows retreat from the light slower than they should have, sliding back along the stones like serpents. Shapes churned in the darkness when Barend pulled his torch away again, things that looked like faces and hands in Johann's imagination. He shuddered and tried to get a hold of himself. There was nothing there, he told himself. Nothing.

At the far end of the hall was a big, throne-like wooden chair, each armrest ending in a carved, roaring lion's head. It sat across from a cold marble fireplace, and above the mantle was an enormous, bronze-framed mirror, its glass smeared dark with dirt and dust, the crossed axes of the House of Karnstock adorning each corner. Off to one side of the hall, a grand staircase led up to a second-floor balcony that ran the width of the room.

"There's no one here," Edwin said.

"Upstairs," Luther said. "We all saw the light in the tower. He's here. I know it."

Staying at the rear of the group as they climbed the steps, Johann heard a soft whispering behind him. He turned and once again saw nothing but shadows that seemed to slither and grope. He clutched his Bible closer.

"Did you hear that?" he whispered.

Directly ahead of him, Henry Maentel replied, "Hear what?"

"Voices," Johann said. He glanced over the banister. "Whispers."

Henry stopped and listened. "I don't hear anything."

Johann didn't hear anything either. The sound had died away, and now the shadows sat motionless.

"It's only your nerves," Henry said, and started climbing the steps again.

But Johann felt it in the way his skin prickled—it was more than just nerves. Something was here with them.

The steps ended at the balcony, part of a long corridor lined with doors. Barend looked up and down the corridor, and said, "I don't see another staircase. How are we supposed to get up to the tower?"

"The stairs must be behind one of these doors," Luther said. He opened the first one, and Barend poked his torch inside, revealing only an empty, cobwebbed room. Johann thought he saw the shadows shrink back fitfully from the torchlight.

Shrill, hissing whispers filled the air, and this time everyone heard them. "What is that?" Barend asked, wincing at the sound.

"Spirits," Johann said, clutching his cross. "He's filled this castle with the spirits of the dead."

"Ignore it—just get these doors open!" Luther ordered.

They lined up in front of the doors, each taking one and opening them in succession, but all they found were more empty rooms. When Johann's turn came, he let go of his cross and pulled the dagger from his boot. Taking a deep breath, he turned the knob and opened the door. Without a torch of his own, there was only darkness on the other side, but he could tell this room was different. Where the others had a stale odor of dust and mold, this room gave off a headier scent, the sweet rot of old meat. It was the smell of a charnel house, carried to him on a cool breeze that shouldn't be coming from a windowless room.

Christian Hillenbrand appeared next to him, scratching his red beard nervously. "Your torch," Johann said. Christian tipped the flame into the room.

The room was circular in shape, its walls and floor fashioned from bare stone. Shackles on long chains had been bolted to the walls, two up high, two at the floor, all along the circumference of the room. He noticed one set was broken—the top chain had been pulled out of the wall and the wrist cuffs smashed open against the floor. Someone had escaped.

Ava Hillenbrand—had she been the one to pull the chain free? Johann thought back to the night Ava returned to the village. After the doctor, Hahn Gehrig, had been unable to discern what was ailing her, Johann had watched over her while she thrashed violently in her bed, sweating and groaning and vomiting up a thick white substance he hadn't recognized. He remembered her voice, hoarse and low, when she'd started raving, "Leave me alone...get out of my head...I won't let you!" He'd held Ava's clammy hand and asked what she meant, but she was too delirious to hear him. "This body is mine," she said, and died shortly before morning.

Christian shouted for the others to come see what they'd found, pulling Johann from his memories. He was grateful to let them go. The men came running, and Johann followed them into the room, the cool breeze chilling the nervous sweat on his back. The draft, he realized, was coming from a round pit in the center of the room. He stepped around the dark hole and took a closer look at the room around him. The stone walls were stained with dried blood and the chalky remains of a strange white substance. The same unnatural ichor that Ava had vomited up, he assumed. The same that had stained the cobblestone white when she bled on it. He glanced over at Christian Hillenbrand and saw he was thinking the same thing: What had happened to his daughter in this room?

Edwin was the first to say it, though most of them were already thinking it. "They're dead. I knew it. This is where he killed them all."

But Luther shook his head. "Dora is still here, somewhere in the castle. I can feel it."

The hissing whispers came again, louder than before, piercing Johann's skull like needles. He fell to his knees, dropped the dagger and Bible, and covered his ears. The others winced and stumbled in confusion. Johann squeezed his eyes shut, trying to silence the voices. They were filled with such hatred and fury that he felt himself being swept up in the emotion, gritting his teeth and banging his fists against the sides of his head.

When he opened his eyes, the room seemed darker, as if the torches had dimmed. But it wasn't the torches, he realized in horror, it was the shadows. They were growing, overpowering the light. Thick black vines of shadow reached out for them. He squeezed his eyes shut again and heard one of the men near him scream, a hoarse, wet sound that cut off suddenly. He heard cries of confusion, the sound of blades cutting uselessly through the air, rifle shots ricocheting off the stone walls, and more screams. He felt fingers brushing his face, icy and sharp.

He forced his eyes open. Shadows filled the room, lashing from the walls like tentacles, wrapping around men and dragging them into the dark corners. The whispers were deafening. Shapes moved within the shadows, grinning skulls and clawed hands, but his mind fought to reject the images. This couldn't be happening.

Someone grabbed his shoulder from behind. He flinched and cried out, but then he heard Barend's voice.

"Father, are you all right?" Barend reached under his arms and helped him to his feet. "We're boxed in, we can't—"

A thick black wall of shadow passed between them, knocking Barend to the floor. The shadows swirled over the big man, and Johann caught a glimpse of a bony hand slashing Barend's left cheek, leaving a deep red cut. Another cry caught his attention, and Johann turned to see a column of shadows dragging Christian Hillenbrand toward the wall. Frozen in fear, he expected to hear Christian slam into the stones, but instead he vanished into the dark as if the wall weren't there.

This couldn't be happening.

Henry, still gripping his rifle, was pulled up into the air and spun around like a toy. His boot struck Johann's cheek, and as the priest fell backward, Henry screamed and tumbled to the floor, bouncing off the edge of the pit and disappearing into the darkness below. Johann scrabbled for the dagger he'd dropped, then slashed at the shadows all around him, but the blade only passed through them harmlessly.

The shadows, and the shapes inside, groped for him. A wispy tendril touched the silver cross around his neck and jerked back suddenly. The deafening whispers turned into screeches of pain. Thinking quickly, Johann dropped the dagger and grabbed the cross with both hands, holding it out before him as far as the chain would allow. The shadows pulled back, shrieking. He rose to his feet and turned in a circle with the cross. The shadows around him thrashed and recoiled. His throat hurt, he realized suddenly, a raw, shredding pain, and only then did he realize he was still screaming in terror.

The shadows retreated, disappearing like smoke into the cracks between the stones. The light from the remaining torches flared brightly again. Laughing with relief, Johann kissed the cross and clasped it tight.

Barend sat up from the floor, wiping blood from the deep wound on his cheek. Luther and Edwin glanced around in confusion.

"Where are the others?" Luther asked.

Johann stopped laughing. Ten men had entered the room, he remembered, but now there were only four. Yet there were no bodies anywhere. The shadows must have dragged the others away, he realized, just like they'd done to Christian Hillenbrand. Pulled them into the darkness. "They're dead," he said.

Barend stood up, shaking his head in disbelief. "All of them?"

"Not all," a voice answered. It was Henry's voice, echoing from deep inside the pit. They gathered around the edge and peered down into the inky blackness. "I hurt my knee," Henry said. "I think I can walk, but I'm going to need some help getting out of here."

"Hang on," Edwin called down. He turned to the others. "It looks deep. We'll need a rope."

"There's a tunnel down here, too," Henry called up to them. "I can feel the air moving. It's cold and it smells rank, but at least that means it leads somewhere. Toss down a torch and let's see."

Luther dropped his torch into the pit. It spiraled down through the darkness and landed on a dirt floor twenty-five feet below. Henry picked up the torch, the flickering flame illuminating his face. "Don't go anywhere," Luther called down to him. "I don't know if the shadows, or whatever they were, are coming back."

"Then I suggest you hurry," Henry replied.

They didn't have a rope, so they cut the chains out of their moorings on the walls, knotted them together, and secured one end to a thick metal bolt in the floor. Using the shackles as hand- and footholds, all four of them climbed down into the pit.

Henry's knee was raw and bloody, but he could stand. "Took you long enough," he said. He strapped his rifle across his back and pulled tentatively on the chains to see if they would hold him. "So, who gets to lift me up on his shoulders?"

"Hold on," Edwin said. He went to the wall, where the pitch-black mouth of a tunnel opened into the pit. "Where do you think it leads?"

Barend sniffed the air. "It smells like an abattoir."

"You don't need to tell me," Henry said. "I've been breathing it longer than you have."

From deep inside the tunnel came the sound of a heavy object sliding along the dirt. Edwin jumped back. "Something's in there," he said. They heard it again, a sound like dragging footsteps. "It's coming this way!"

Henry pulled his rifle off his back. Johann gripped his cross tightly and stared into the tunnel. As the shuffling grew closer, an important question occurred to him too late. Why would the Necromancer have a pit in the middle of the room where he tortured his victims? The only purpose it could serve was as a place to throw their remains when he was done with them, but there were no bodies on the floor, no bones.

A shape appeared in the mouth of the tunnel. Johann and the others backed away. The figure kept to the shadows, but pale white fingers, their nails crusty and black, gripped the stone wall at the edge of the tunnel. Edwin leveled his torch, and the flickering orange light revealed a boy in his late teens, tall, skinny, and as pale as fresh snow. His lips had been sewn together with thick wire. Slabs of metal had been bolted to parts of his flesh, and forklike tines covered his eyes.

"You poor child," Johann said, stepping forward. "What have they done to you? We can help. We can get you out of here." The boy tilted his head at the sound of his voice, and Johann realized he was blind. He took another step closer. "Are there others like you who need help?"

The boy grabbed Johann and wrapped his fingers around the priest's neck. His grip was as cold and hard as iron. The boy's throat bobbed as he tried to giggle, a string of drool escaping between the metal stitches in his lips. Johann couldn't break away. He felt dizzy and desperate for air. He realized he shouldn't have let go of the cross. If he survived this day, he promised God he'd never let go of it again.

Barend grabbed him, trying to pull him back while Luther pried the boy's fingers off his neck. Johann fell to the floor, coughing and massaging his throat. The boy groped for Luther's face. Henry stepped up, cocking the double hammers on his rifle, and aimed at the boy. The boy lurched forward, and the torchlight revealed a dark port-wine stain on the side of his face. A birthmark. Johann recognized it right away, and turned to Henry in horror.

Henry Maentel lowered the gun. "Abelard?" he said. It was barely a whisper. The boy jerked abruptly toward the sound of Henry's voice. "Son, is that—is that really you?"

"Shoot it!" Edwin cried. "Look at it, man! Are you blind? It's not your boy anymore!"

Henry ignored him. "You're alive," he said, as the thing groped toward him. "I thought you were dead. All these years, you were still here. Alive."

"Henry, don't be a fool!" Johann rasped. "Take it down!"

The thing that had once been Abelard Maentel reached blindly for his father's face.

Edwin dropped his torch, grabbed the rifle out of Henry's limp hands, and aimed for Abelard's head. The boy, hearing the sudden movement, turned to face him, wrapping two worm-white fingers around the barrel. Edwin squeezed the trigger, obliterating half of Abelard's hand and putting a big wet hole in the boy's head. Johann winced as blood and bone spattered his clothes.

Abelard fell. Stunned, Henry dropped to his knees beside the body of his son. He touched it, then yanked his hand away. "You're—you're so cold." He shook his head. "What did he do to you?"

Luther put a hand on his shoulder. "Henry..."

"What did that monster do to my boy?" Henry raged, sobbing.

His cry brought a reply from inside the tunnel. Moans echoed off the walls, and the sound of more feet dragging along the dirt floor.

"There's more of them," Barend said. "We have to get out of here, now!"

Johann stood, picked up the torch Edwin had dropped, and moved to the mouth of the tunnel for a better look. The light didn't penetrate very far, but he could sense them out there, dozens of them, maybe more. The stench of rotting meat was overpowering.

They dragged Henry away from his son's body, then helped him up the makeshift rope. They climbed up after him, one at a time. Johann went last, and his muscles ached as he wrapped his legs around the chains and pulled himself up with one hand while holding the torch with the other. When he reached the top, the others grabbed him and pulled him quickly over the edge and onto the floor of the torture chamber. Luther pulled the chain up quickly so nothing could follow them. Johann looked down into the pit. He heard figures shuffling below, saw chalk-white hands groping up out of the darkness.

Beside him, Barend asked, "Is this what the Necromancer did to the ones he took?"

"I hope not all of them," Johann said.

Barend stared at the pale, grasping hands below. "Do you—do you think Rebekah is down there? Is she one of them now? If Henry's boy was changed, she..." He trailed off, his breath hitching.

Johann pulled Barend away from the pit. "Don't torture yourself with such thoughts."

Barend squeezed his eyes shut. "I can't help it. It's all I can see in my mind."

Johann found his Bible and dagger on the floor and picked them up. "She's at peace now, Barend. The things down there aren't alive. They're only empty shells, the Necromancer's puppets, nothing more."

Barend turned away. "I can't bear to think of her like that."

"Then don't," Luther said. He picked up a fallen musket and tossed it to Barend. "Have your vengeance instead."

Behind Luther, Henry nodded in silent assent, still stunned at what he'd seen.

Luther led them out onto the second-floor balcony. Finally, behind a door at the end of the hallway, they found a carpeted staircase winding upward in a tight spiral to the tower where they'd seen the lighted window. Flickering oil lamps lined the walls, so they left their torches in the rack at the bottom of the steps before they started climbing. Johann heard the low buzz of whispers in his ear. He glanced back, but the shadows didn't move. He touched his cross and wondered if they were scared of him now that he'd found a way to hurt them.

At the top of the stairs was a small landing, the walls, ceiling, and floor all fashioned from a pristine marble. An impossibly white door stood before them, and above it, fastened to the wall, were two crossed silver axes. A light shone through the crack under the door.

Johann's palms felt sweaty. He looked down to make sure the hilt of the dagger was still visible in his boot. Next to him, Henry and Barend readied their guns. Edwin drew his blade. Luther, sword in hand, kicked open the door. The light that poured from inside was so bright it blinded them.

A voice so cold and hollow it seemed to come from everywhere said, "Hello, Luther."

16.

Inside the stable, Johann sat on his bed of straw and stared up at the ceiling. In the evening light, a dark stain was barely visible on the wooden boards above him, a stain that hadn't been there before. Was it Barend's blood, he wondered? His friend had been murdered in the room right above his head last night, and Johann had slept through it.

Or had he? He'd woken on the steps of the church, not in the stable. Who knew what had happened in the time between? Had he witnessed the murder? Seen the killer's face without knowing it? He thought of the times he'd woken with fresh cuts on his hands, blood on the silver cross around his neck, and wondered if the truth might be even worse than that.

The mare in the next stall eyed him over the low wall and snorted.

"No, that's impossible," he told the horse. "I couldn't have killed Barend. Or Edwin. Why would I?"

The horse's head dipped out of sight, then returned with a mouthful of hay.

"The voices from the castle?" Johann asked. "They torment me, yes. They try to break my will. But control my actions without my knowledge? How could that be? I'm still wearing the cross." The horse chewed disinterestedly. "Yes, you're quite right, my friend. The birds let me pass unharmed today, but that's because they remember me from the castle. That's why they didn't attack. They remembered *this*." He tugged on the silver cross. The horse bent for more hay, restlessly stamping a hoof. "No," Johann insisted. "It's because they fear the power of the cross. I'm not in league with them. I'm not in the castle's service. I'm my own man!"

The mare snorted and turned away. In the recesses of Johann's mind, the voices laughed at him.

"I'm my own man," he said again softly.

The mare whinnied suddenly and tossed her mane. Her eyes widened, and her nostrils flared. Johann heard a footstep beyond the closed gate of his stall. He stood up to see, but it was too dark. The other horses in the stable joined the mare in her panic, snorting and kicking at the walls. Johann opened the shuttered window behind him to let in the moonlight, then turned back to the gate just in time to see it swing open.

A young woman entered his stall. She wore a white nightgown and her feet were bare. She smiled at him and tucked a lock of straight brown hair behind one ear. "Hello, Father."

Johann squinted at her. She looked familiar, but he couldn't quite place her. The child of a congregation member, maybe? She couldn't be more than nineteen.

"Don't you know me, Father?" she asked.

He shook his head. Something about the way she asked that question frightened him.

She took a step toward him. "Don't you remember watching over me as I slept in my bed, burning with fever?"

He backed away from her. He squeezed his eyes shut, certain he was dreaming, but when he opened them she was still there. "Ava," he whispered, a cold sweat breaking on his brow. "But you died that night. I saw."

"That's not all you saw," the Hillenbrand girl said. Her voice cut through him like an icy wind. She lifted one strap of her nightgown and slid it off her shoulder. "You enjoyed watching me, didn't you? The way I tossed aside the covers when I grew too hot. The way the sweat made my nightgown stick to my skin as I writhed and moaned in my fever. It aroused you, didn't it? Tell me something, Father. Did you give in to temptation that night? It would have been so easy with no one else in the room. Did you touch me while I slept?" She slipped the strap off her other shoulder, and the nightgown pooled around her feet. "Would you like to touch me now?"

Johann shook his head, trying not to look at her naked body. "You're not here. You can't be."

"I'm here because you want me to be here," she said, moving toward him.

"No, that's not true." He retreated another step and his back hit the wall. "I'm not in league with darkness. I'm my own man!"

"I'm here because you never stopped thinking about me." She was so close he could feel the warmth of her body. She put a hand on his chest and leaned in close. "Why do you think that is, Father? What was it about me that was so unforgettable?"

Her lips brushed his, her breath hot against his face. Johann pushed her away and lifted his silver cross. "You're not Ava! You're from the castle, a shadow pretending to be a girl!"

She laughed, wrapped her fingers around the cross, and pushed his hand down gently. "Why would this old thing frighten me?"

Johann stared. It was impossible. The cross had repelled the shadows before. Touching it had caused them pain. It should have affected her the same way. Unless—unless she wasn't one of them, unless she was real. But no, Ava Hillenbrand was dead. He'd seen her die that night. The Necromancer could commune with spirits, he could reanimate corpses with the help of magic and metal, but not like this. She didn't look anything like the creatures in the pit. Her hand, her breath—she was *warm*. It was a human being that stood before him, but not Ava. Surely not Ava. Someone who could make him think he was seeing Ava, then. An illusion. But who had that kind of power? The Necromancer was dead.

And yet...had he seen the Necromancer's body? Had any of them? Only Luther claimed to have seen the Necromancer die.

The edges of Ava's body softened, blurring and fanning out in a heavy mist. Another illusion. The horses whinnied and kicked the walls again, shaking the stable so violently it was as if an avalanche were coming down around it. Johann reached into his belt for Fritz Gruber's hunting knife, but his hand came back empty. It must have fallen out when he'd laid down for the night. He saw it sitting on the straw by his feet and snatched it up quickly.

Something inside the mist glinted an eerie silver, and he saw a figure coming toward him. Startled, he tried to take a step back but forgot he was already against the wall. He lost his footing and fell to the floor. The figure was almost upon him. Lying on his back, Johann started to raise the knife.

The whoosh of something heavy swinging through the air reached his ears too late. A silver axe head came down on his wrist, shearing through it and into the wooden floor beneath him. Numb with shock, he stared at the bloody stump at the end of his arm. His hand lay on the other side of the axe, its twitching fingers loosening their grip on the hunting knife.

The blood-spattered axe rocked back and forth until it came loose from the floor, then lifted away into the fog again. Johann grabbed his cross with his remaining hand. The mist churned, thinning for a moment, and he looked up into the face of the one who had come to murder him.

"Luther should have killed you when he had the chance," Johann said.

The axe came down again.

17.

Standing in the center of one of Helmburg's streets, that peculiar sense of duality hit Kasch again. Some part of him knew he was sleeping peacefully under the covers of his bed, but he was also awake, standing on dew-slick cobblestones, a low-hanging mist playing around his boots. The mysterious woman was there too, wearing a flowing white gown trimmed with royal blue at the neck and sleeves. A gentle breeze ruffled her honey-colored hair.

Fleeting memories like fractured shards of a mirror spun through his mind—fainting on the street, being carried back to the house, someone removing his shoes and putting him in bed. These events he was certain of, even if he couldn't wholly remember them, but whatever had happened after that was lost to the blackout. All he knew was that he'd woken alone sometime in the night, confused and frightened, convinced that nightmarish figures of pale flesh and metal were gathering in the dark outside his window. In a moment of courage, he'd gone out to investigate and found himself here, in the middle of the village, with her. Her pale skin was so translucent it glowed in the moonlight.

"You've come to me every night, and I don't even know your name," Kasch said, then immediately cursed his foolishness. He'd lost himself in the moment, forgetting this was only a dream. More lucid and vivid than others, perhaps, but a dream nonetheless. She didn't have a name because she wasn't real.

And knowing she wasn't real, Kasch let his gaze move shamelessly along the curves of her body.

"Come," she said, holding out her hand. Her smile highlighted the little birthmark beside her mouth, and stoked the desire inside him.

He took her hand and pulled her toward him to embrace her,

but she resisted. "Let's go back to the house. I want to make love to you," he said, far bolder in the dream than he would ever dare be in true life.

She pulled away from him and said, "You will have everything you want in due time."

He didn't like this. Wasn't he supposed to be in control of his own dreams? Why *shouldn't* they make love?

"Walk with me," she said.

"Walk where?" he asked, annoyed.

"Do you love me?"

"Yes," he said, and was surprised by how much he meant it. When he was with her, he couldn't feel the awful, crushing weight of this place anymore.

His head hurt suddenly. The pain was excruciating, as if his brain were splitting apart. He closed his eyes and tried to stifle the pain.

"Then show me," she said. "Do you remember what I gave you that first night?"

Kasch opened his eyes. To his surprise, he was sitting naked in the stream behind his house, little red fish swimming in a cloud all around him. The water should have been freezing against his bare skin, he knew, but he didn't feel anything. The tiny red fish surrounded him, so many of them he couldn't separate one from another. They flowed past him in the current and disappeared downstream. He had the strangest sense that he had done this before, bathed in this same stream with its curious red fish every night.

"Good boy," the woman said, standing on the grass by the stream. "You won't try to leave again, will you?"

"No," he said. But even in the dream he knew he was lying.

"Because if you leave, we can't be together," she said. "You know that."

Kasch turned to look through the window of the house, and saw himself sleeping in the bed.

"You need me," she said. "I know you feel it. No one else can free the man inside you. You belong here, with me. The two halves must become whole."

He turned back to her. Behind her, figures stood in the dark, their skin glinting like metal.

18.

Sunlight was already pouring through the bedroom window when Kasch woke up. He'd slept later than he wanted to, but he didn't feel rested. He felt tired, drained, and as soon as the fogginess of sleep left his head, the memory of what happened on the thoroughfare came rushing back—the terrifying things he'd seen when he touched the cobblestone, the voice he'd heard that knew his name.

He was certain the experience had been nothing more than a product of his own mind as the blackout came upon him, but that was little comfort. The blackouts were becoming more frequent. It had something to do with Helmburg, he knew. His condition was connected to this place. He hadn't had a single blackout in Bern until the appearance of Otto Gruber, the boy from Helmburg, and that seemed to have triggered it. Now, since his return, he'd had one every day.

He walked through the sitting room and into the hallway, heading toward the front door. A sudden coldness came over him, as if he'd stepped barefoot on a patch of ice. The cold moved through him like a wind.

Behind him, the rustle of cloth. He turned in time to see a flash of white rounding the corner of the sitting room, trailing along the floor like the hem of a dress. His skin tightened along his scalp. Someone else was in the house.

"Hello?" He walked back to the sitting room. "Is someone there?" He circled the marble table at its center, but the room was empty.

The cold came again, icy fingers crawling up his back, and he spun around. A door on the other side of the sitting room closed silently, the door that led to the parlor—a room Luther had forbidden him to enter as a child. Kasch took a deep breath and opened the door. Something white fluttered at him, startling him, but it was just one of the sheets covering the furniture inside, moving in the draft from the door.

There was no one in the parlor. Either he was dreaming or he was going mad.

Why had his father kept him out of this room? He couldn't remember. Probably it was just another of his father's arbitrary commands, born of too much ale and not enough care. But he was the master of the house now, not his father. The old rules had died with him. Kasch walked through the rows of shrouded objects and, with bitter determination, began pulling off sheets one by one, as if by doing so he could uncover every secret his father had kept from him, every secret Helmburg was *still* keeping from him. The furniture beneath the sheets was nicer than in the rest of the house, he noticed, somehow more feminine. As he pulled away another sheet, he uncovered a shelf full of glass figurines. He picked up the slight, delicate statuette of a whirling dancer with scarves in her hands. Such an item could only have belonged to his mother, he thought. The parlor must have been her sanctuary. He looked around the room again with fresh eyes, but everything he saw drove home just how little he knew about her. He carefully replaced the delicate little dancer on the shelf and cursed his father for keeping so much from him.

There was a small fireplace at the far end of the room, and above it a long sheet covered a painting mounted on the wall. He crossed to it, grabbed the corner of the sheet, and pulled. It fluttered down from the canvas and landed at his feet.

Beneath it was a portrait. On the left stood his father, dressed in his best clothes, looking slim and young, his beard neatly trimmed. On the right was a woman with almond-shaped eyes and honey-colored hair that flowed from a widow's peak above her forehead. A small birthmark sat beside her lips.

The likeness knocked the wind out of him. Kasch took a step back, then another. His knees threatened to give out under him.

"It's beautiful, isn't it? I always liked that portrait," a voice behind him said. Kasch turned to see Hahn standing in the doorway. "Forgive my intrusion. I came by to see how you are. I heard you had a bit of a spell in the street yesterday. I trust you're feeling better?"

Kasch turned back to the portrait, unable to speak.

Hahn came into the room and gazed at the painting. "Your parents sat for it shortly after they were married. It took six days to complete. They hated every minute of it. Luther was never good at sitting still, and Dora hated when he fidgeted."

Kasch looked again at the woman standing beside his father. He shuddered thinking about the things he'd said to her in his dreams, the way he'd thought of her. But how could he have given the woman in his dreams his mother's face? He'd never met his mother, hadn't even seen a likeness of her until now.

"I want to apologize for how I acted yesterday," Hahn continued. "I was upset and not myself. I shouldn't have raised my voice at you. Let me make it up by treating you to breakfast at the tavern."

Kasch nodded, suddenly desperate to get away from the portrait. He let Hahn guide him out of the house. He felt tainted, a repulsive thing in the guise of a man. Walking along the thoroughfare toward Huetten's Bierbrunnen, he barely heard Hahn's idle chatter. As they passed a side street, panicked voices caught his attention. A crowd had gathered in front of one of the stables. A moment later, the alarm bell sounded and constables pushed their way through.

An old woman waddled toward them out of the crowd, her white hair tied in a tight bun. Kasch recognized her as the same woman he'd met outside Edwin Roebling's house.

"Frau Nüsseler," Hahn said. "What happened here?"

"It's dreadful, Hahn," she said. "Father Vierick…Johann, he's been murdered."

"Johann?" Hahn's voice was thick with dread. He looked at the constables moving in and out of the stable. "Oh, God. Not him too."

Frau Nüsseler clucked her tongue. "Chopped to pieces just like the others."

The streets and sidewalks of the main thoroughfare had been thoroughly cleaned after the blackbirds departed, leaving no trace of the bloody violence that had occurred there only a day ago. The tavern had been similarly tended to, the floor swept of molted feathers and the shards of broken plates and steins, until only the boards over the broken window gave any indication that the birds had gotten inside. Helmburg was all too good at disguising the truth, Kasch thought.

He pushed his plate of fried eggs away. He had no appetite. He couldn't get the portrait out of his mind, the face of his mother. Remembering how he'd tried to pull her to him made his cheeks burn with shame.

Hahn, shaken by the news of Johann's death, wasn't eating either, and so they sat across from each other, neither eating, and neither speaking.

Finally, Kasch said, "Tell me about—about my mother." His shame was turning to such utter humiliation he had to force the words out of his mouth.

Hahn cleared his throat. "I didn't know Dora very well," he said. "No one did. She wasn't born in Helmburg, and when she came here she mostly kept to herself. Even after she married your father, she was a mystery to us."

"The Necromancer took her," Kasch said. "That much I know."

Hahn nodded. "And your father risked everything to go after her. But there were rumors. That's what I've been worried about telling you. I don't even know if they're worth repeating."

"Tell me," Kasch said.

Hahn stared at his cooling breakfast. "Some said Dora wasn't taken. That she went to the Necromancer willingly."

Kasch furrowed his brow. "What?"

"You have to understand, Helmburg is a small village, isolated by the mountains. We're still old-fashioned, we have our own ways and customs and beliefs. There are people here who don't trust outsiders, and your mother was an outsider."

"Wait, Hahn, what are you implying?"

The old man sighed. "Adultery," he said.

Kasch shook his head. "I don't believe that."

"Gossip doesn't have to be believed to spread," Hahn said. "The truth is, no one knows what happened in that castle. The survivors of Black Easter—Luther, Johann, Barend, Henry, and Edwin—they came back as tight as brothers. They never spoke to anyone else about what went on inside those walls. Dora claimed not to remember any of it. But the rumor took on a life of its own. More and more people came to believe it. In the months after they brought your mother back from the castle, there were…incidents. No one wanted her here."

Kasch remembered the word carved into the windowsill behind his house. *Whore.* It felt like he was being ground down under an immense stone. The more he learned, the more he wished he'd never come back to Helmburg. He hated this place.

"Luther never wavered in his love for her. After she died, he took the loss hard. Started drinking more." Hahn shook his head. "I think after a while he couldn't handle trying to raise you on his own, so he sent you away to those schools in Switzerland."

"You're lying," Kasch said with a bitter smile. "If that was the reason he sent me away, he wouldn't have cut off contact. He wouldn't have made sure nobody informed me when he died. He never wanted me to come back to Helmburg, Hahn. Why?"

The old man exhaled a shaky breath. "I don't know."

"Just stop," Kasch said. "Everyone has lied to me since I got here. You, the Bürgermeister, Barend. You've all been keeping something from me, but I have a right to know."

Hahn poked a fork at his cold eggs. "Let's just eat our breakfast and leave the past where it belongs."

"You know the real reason, don't you? It wasn't because he couldn't raise me alone. It wasn't for the sake of my education, or any of the other things I told myself so I wouldn't hate him too much."

"Stop this." Hahn shut his eyes, as if he could make Kasch disappear.

"Hahn, look at me," he said. "All my life, I've wondered if I did something wrong, if anyone cared about me at all. I need to know the truth. I need to know why my father treated me the way he did."

Hahn opened his eyes and sighed. "Luther didn't think you were his."

The words were like a punch in the stomach. Kasch sat back, trying to weather the storm of emotions blowing through him. Not Luther's son? Johann had asked him whose blood ran in his veins. He'd dismissed it as the nonsensical ravings of a lunatic, but now… No, it was a mistake, a stupid rumor in a paranoid little village. *Of course* Luther was his father.

"Did you really want to hear that? Does it make you happier?"

Hahn asked bitterly. He took his napkin off his lap and threw it on the table like a white flag of surrender. "You were born nine months after Luther brought your mother back from Castle Karnstock. All the whispers about her extramarital activities, can you imagine what torture it must have been for him after he risked his life to go get her? It's no wonder he numbed himself with drink."

"My father..." Kasch paused. Father? The word had no meaning for him anymore. The word was a joke. "Luther really thought I wasn't his?"

"He didn't think that at first, but as you grew older..." Hahn shook his head. "You looked so much like your mother, but your coloring, your hair..."

"I didn't look enough like Luther, you mean," Kasch said.

The old man nodded. "I suppose he thought that if you stayed, you might follow in the Necromancer's footsteps. But if you were far from this place, you would never know about the Necromancer, or your mother, or any of it. So he sent you away."

He pictured Johann jabbing a bony finger at him. *You shouldn't have come back, boy. Bad things will happen.* The old priest wasn't the only madman in Helmburg. They all were. Their superstitious paranoia had forced him from his family, his home, and any chance he might have had for a normal life.

"He should have just killed me," Kasch said, slumping in his chair. "He could have saved all the money he spent on tuition."

"Luther would never do that," Hahn said. "You can't raise a boy for thirteen years without growing attached. I should know, my boy died at about that age. I couldn't bring myself to have another. I told my wife there was no point in it, that if we had another child he only would die too, either from illness or at the hands of the Necromancer, and I couldn't live through that again. The look of disgust on her face when I told her that..." He shook his head. "She left me, and now I'm just a sad old man living alone in the same village I was born in, and most likely will die in. We all make choices in life, my boy. They're not always good ones or right ones, but we have to live with the consequences."

"So what do you think?" Kasch asked, trying to sound brave. "Whose son am I?"

"You're Luther's son," Hahn said. "You have to be." He tried to smile, but it looked forced. Hahn was scared of him, Kasch realized, and he hated the old man for it. Like Johann, Hahn wasn't certain whose blood ran in Kasch's veins, no matter what he said. And that made Kasch wonder, too.

There had been five survivors of the raid on Castle Karnstock. One, Luther, had drunk himself to death months ago. Three others, Edwin, Barend, and Johann, had been murdered. There was only one man left who knew his mother. Only one who knew what happened at the castle, and only one who could tell him the truth.

Was he the son of a hero, or the son of a monster?

19.

BLACK EASTER, 1826

Henry Maentel looked away from the brightly lit room at the top of the tower and struggled to slide new shells into his rifle, but his hands were shaking too much. Even when he finally loaded the rifle and snapped it shut, his feet felt like they were nailed to the floor. Sweat dripped down his sides like cold fingers brushing his ribs, chilling him. He swallowed hard, lifted the rifle, and forced himself to follow the others into the room.

Inside, the floor, walls, and ceiling were all stark white. There were no lamps or candles, at least none that he could see. The dazzling light seemed to be emanating from the walls themselves. In the center of the room, Dora Möllhausen, dressed in a white gown with royal-blue trim around the neck and sleeves, lay on a granite slab that Henry at first thought was positioned on the floor, but then realized was actually, impossibly, hovering several inches above it. Dora's eyes were closed, and her hands were folded over her stomach. He thought she was dead until he saw her chest rising and falling.

When Henry was a boy, he'd met Baron Karnstock, the original occupant of this castle. Before the Baron and his family disappeared, they used to come down from the mountainside to spend time in Helmburg. The man standing next to Dora, facing them with a confident smile, was the Baron. Henry was sure of it. He had the same tall stature and sharp, regal features, the same piercing black eyes under heavy brows and slick, black hair. And yet, everything about the way he stood, the way he carried himself, was different. Where once he had seemed so kindly and mannered to the young

Henry, he now gave off a dark presence that filled the room. Henry felt a chill when those coal-black eyes met his. The rifle shook in his hands. This man, the Necromancer, looked like the Baron, but he wasn't the Baron.

"Henry," Luther ordered, not taking his eyes off the Necromancer, "you and the others get Dora out of here. Take her downstairs and wait for me."

Henry moved warily toward the slab on which Dora rested. He kept his rifle trained on the Necromancer.

"She stays here," the Necromancer said. His voice was like a thousand dead men speaking as one, and Henry fought the urge to scream.

He shook Dora's shoulder gently, trying to wake her. Her eyes stayed closed. Henry shook again, harder, but she didn't stir. "Something's wrong with her," he said.

The Necromancer waved his hand, and a force as strong as hurricane winds blew Henry off his feet. He slid backward on the floor until he hit the wall, his injured knee flaring with pain. "She stays here," the Necromancer said again.

Luther stepped forward, his sword pointed at the Necromancer's chest. "What have you done to my wife?"

"She serves a greater purpose now than the wife of a farrier," the Necromancer said.

Luther advanced on him. "You bewitched her. You've done something to her mind."

The Necromancer laughed, and the sound of it was like wind blowing through a tomb.

Henry stood up, trying to ignore the sharp pain in his knee. He limped over to Edwin, Johann, and Barend. While Luther distracted the Necromancer, Henry nodded toward Dora, and the others nodded back.

Luther took another step forward, drawing back his sword. Henry and the others seized the moment and ran for Dora. They didn't make it. The Necromancer barely looked at them as they were blown off their feet and across the floor.

The bright light in the walls dimmed, fading to a dark red that tinted everything in the room the color of blood. "Do you understand how easily I could destroy you?" the Necromancer asked. "It would only take a thought, and the dust from your bones would powder this floor." Shadow tendrils bloomed from the darkening corners and snaked through the air.

Henry struggled to his feet and lifted his rifle, unsure whether to point it at the Necromancer or the gathering shadows. Next to him, Johann grabbed his cross and whispered the Lord's Prayer over and over. It only made Henry more nervous. His heart drummed in his ears, and though his mouth went dry, the rest of him felt sopping with sweat. He drew back from the tendrils, but his injured knee buckled. His sweaty finger jerked against the double triggers of his rifle, and the loud crack of the gunshot startled him. Two holes burst open in the Necromancer's shoulder, knocking him back a step. No blood sprayed from the wound. Instead, a thick white grue oozed out and down his shirt.

On the slab, Dora groaned in her sleep, her brow furrowing.

The room shook with the Necromancer's rage. The shadows lashed out, slamming Henry against the wall and pinning him there. His rifle clattered to the floor. Arms reached for him within the shadow, bony fingers scratching at him. His breath hitching in terror, he wondered if he was going to die, and if the Necromancer would turn him into one of those hideous creatures in the pit.

The twin wounds in the Necromancer's shoulder filled with white ichor, then sealed closed as if they'd never existed. Johann sprang forward, brandishing his silver cross like a weapon. The shadows shrieked and cleared a path, but the Necromancer simply reached out and grabbed the priest by the head. His long fingers sank effortlessly, bloodlessly into Johann's temples. Thin columns of shadow raced forward, tracing along the Necromancer's fingers and disappearing into Johann's skull. The priest screamed.

When the Necromancer released him, Johann fell to his knees, clutching his head. "Get them out!" he cried. "Get them out of my head!"

The crack from Barend Lang's musket echoed through the room. The Necromancer raised his hand, and the musket ball stopped in midair and burst apart into dust. "This game no longer amuses me," he said. More shadows sprang from the walls, filling the room with a writhing darkness that pinned Barend, Luther, and Edwin against the walls, just like Henry. Claws within the shadows shredded their shirts to get at their skin.

From where he knelt, Johann pulled the dagger out of his boot and thrust it upward, stabbing it into the Necromancer's stomach. The Necromancer cried out, his face twisting in surprise. White ooze spat from his mouth and coated his chin. Johann gripped the hilt of the dagger tightly, but instead of pulling it out, he twisted it and drove it deeper. Henry had never seen such violence from the priest. It took a moment for the shock to clear and for him to understand what Johann had already figured out. The Necromancer couldn't heal the wound if the dagger's blade remained inside him.

On the granite slab that hovered above the floor, Dora groaned again. Her skin glistened with a feverish sweat.

The shadows pulled back with the Necromancer's agony, releasing Henry from their grip. He fell to the floor, wincing, and watched the shadows swirl around the wounded Necromancer, who struggled to keep his footing.

Edwin Roebling grabbed his sword from where it fell and launched himself toward to Necromancer. He plunged the blade through the Necromancer's chest and, following Johann's lead, left it there. The Necromancer howled, doubling over. The room shook again, knocking them all to the floor. The Necromancer fell to his knees. The slab on which Dora laid crashed to the floor and broke in half.

The shadows retreated, and the room brightened. Henry looked for his rifle, but it was gone. So were Barend's musket and Edwin and Luther's swords. The shadows had dragged their weapons away with them.

Johann helped Henry to his feet. "Are you all right?"

"Other than my knee, yes," he said. "What about you, Father?"

Johann blinked and rubbed his temples. "Yes, I—I think so. I could hear them. The shadows, whatever they are. They—they were in my head. They're gone now, I think."

"Take Dora downstairs," Luther ordered. "Quickly."

Barend and Edwin picked Dora up. She hung limply in their arms as they carried her toward the door.

The Necromancer coughed up sticky white droplets. He reached out with one trembling, white-spattered hand, and said, "Release her."

"She's coming back with us," Luther said. "Where she belongs."

"She must stay here," the Necromancer insisted, milky white clumps sluicing from his lips. He wrapped his hands around the hilt of the sword that stuck out of his chest.

"Go!" Luther shouted at the others. Johann helped Edwin and Barend take Dora out of the room. They started down the stairs, but Henry stayed behind a moment, staring at the Necromancer kneeling on the floor. Bleeding. Dying. Groveling. To think he'd been so frightened of this man for so long.

The Necromancer grimaced and started to pull the sword out of his chest. The blade slid out, inch by inch, coated in thick white ooze, and Henry's fear came rushing back to him.

"Get out of here, Henry," Luther said. He walked out of the room to the landing outside, and Henry followed him.

"It's no use, Luther," Henry insisted. "Our weapons are gone. We're defenseless. He'll just keep healing himself."

"Then I'll make it so there's not enough of him left to heal." Luther reached up over the door and pulled one of the crossed silver axes off the wall. "Go, Henry," he said. "Stay with Dora, make sure she's all right. I have to end this." Gripping the axe in one hand, he stalked back into the room.

Henry turned and started down the spiral staircase to catch up with the others, but paused when he heard the Necromancer's voice booming from above. He looked back up the steps, but he'd descended too far to see what was happening inside the room.

"You should have heeded the warning I left for you in the woods," the Necromancer said. "Anyone else would have turned back. But not brave Luther Möllhausen."

"It's over." Luther's voice. "You're nothing now. Just a dying old man."

The Necromancer laughed, an awful sound that made Henry shudder. "Fool. This body has been dying for years. My search for a new one drove me to a harvest some might call ruthless or cruel. I call it survival. But the weak, miserable people of your pathetic village weren't suitable vessels. They couldn't hold my essence. Even after I sewed their mouths shut with wire, it would find ways to break free of their bodies. I would sew their bodies closed again or bolt them back together with metal, but still nothing worked. I have a pit full of rejects for my trouble."

"So you failed," Luther said. "It ends here."

The Necromancer laughed again. It turned into a wet cough. "Go ahead, Luther, strike me down. Destroy this body, it doesn't matter. The seeds of my resurrection have already been planted, and when the time comes your wretched little village will drown in blood."

Henry couldn't listen anymore. He turned and limped down the steps. Outside the castle, he found Johann, Edwin, and Barend sitting on a log in the courtyard. Dora was with them, leaning against Barend, her eyes still closed. "Luther's coming," Henry said. He stopped when he realized how quiet it was. "Where are the men we left outside?" he asked. The others didn't answer him.

He turned around then, and saw them. Five bodies lay on the ground, their clothes torn, their flesh slashed so deeply their skin was slick with blood.

"The birds," Barend explained. "It must have happened while we were inside."

The blackbirds. Henry had almost forgotten about them. He looked to the castle walls, but they were bare. "They're gone," he said.

"Look up," Barend said.

Henry did, and gasped. He'd spoken too soon. The blackbirds circled high above the castle like a spinning black funnel. There must have been hundreds of them.

An agonized cry erupted from the tower like thunder, louder and more terrible than anything he'd heard before. The birds broke their pattern and flew screeching into the night. They were gone before the cry subsided.

Dora screamed suddenly and fell over. Barend grabbed her shoulders and helped her sit upright. Her eyes were open and wide with terror as she glanced around. "Luther!" she cried, panicked. "Where's Luther?"

"Dora, are you all right?" Barend asked.

She struggled against him momentarily, then calmed as she gradually remembered who he was. "Where—where am I, Barend? Where is my husband?"

"He's coming," Barend said. "Everything's all right now."

Edwin shook his head, sneering, and stood up. He spat on the ground and walked away from the log.

Henry followed him. "What is it, Edwin?"

"I've been practicing law for a long time," Edwin whispered. "After a while, you learn to tell when people are lying. It's in their eyes. And this one?" He nodded at Dora. "She's lying."

"What are you saying?" Henry demanded.

"When she vanished, there was no feather left in her place," Edwin said. "She's no victim. She came here of her own volition. She made a cuckold of Luther."

"No, you heard what Luther said. She was bewitched," Henry insisted. "She might have been under the Necromancer's spell the whole time."

"He believes that because he's a good man. It's not in him to imagine she could betray him like this," Edwin said. He clenched his jaw angrily. "We risked our necks for her. Good men lost their lives. We should have left the whore to die."

Luther appeared in the doorway then. Henry flinched, worried he'd heard Edwin, but if he did he gave no sign. The silver axe in his hand was spattered and streaked with white. "The Necromancer is dead," he said. Then he gazed at the bird-ravaged corpses and frowned. "Bring the kindling and oil barrels. I want this place burned to the ground. Let there be nothing left of this abomination." He walked over to Dora. She got up and threw her arms around his neck. He pulled her close with his free hand.

"I don't remember," Dora said. "Not any of it."

"It's all right," Luther said. "Whatever he did, it's over now."

Edwin glanced at Henry, his mouth a hard line. Henry looked away, preferring his version of events to Edwin's, and watched Luther embrace the wife he'd surely rescued from the clutches of a fiend.

Over Luther's shoulder, he saw Dora open her eyes. He wasn't sure what he saw in them, only that suddenly he felt very cold.

20.

The alarm bell had finally stopped tolling by the time Kasch left the tavern. He felt eyes watching him as he walked to Henry Maentel's house, his scalp tingling as villagers peeked out at him from behind curtains and half-opened doors. Some stood on the corners of the thoroughfare or in front of their shops and stopped talking when he passed. Others crossed the street when they saw him coming.

He knew what they were thinking. He could see it in their eyes, feel it in the burn of their stares. The murderer was still at large, and with Johann dead Helmburg needed a new scapegoat. Of course they'd chosen him, the outsider, the prodigal son, the one they'd gossiped about since he was born. The boy whose own father didn't trust him.

Across the street, Fritz Gruber and his blacksmith thugs glared at him, their mouths set in hard lines. The threat in their eyes made him want to walk faster, but he fought the impulse. He wouldn't give them the satisfaction. He belonged in Helmburg as much as they did. For now, anyway. As soon as he had his answers, he would leave this godforsaken village and never come back.

He knocked on the door of Henry's house, and while he waited he glanced back at the street. Everyone was still staring at him. It was only a matter of time before Fritz and his men came after him the way they'd gone after Johann, he was sure. He knocked again, more insistently.

Finally, Liese opened the door, smiling. "Kasch! Are you feeling better? I was worried about you. I hoped you'd come 'round today."

"Your father," he blurted, "is he home?"

She held the door open for him, and he stepped into the grand foyer of the Bürgermeister's house. "No, he's at the stable with the constables. Did you hear what happened to Johann? It's terrible." She closed the door and led him into the living room. "My mother's out too and won't be back for a while. We've got the whole house to ourselves."

"I need to talk to your father," Kasch said. "I should go find him."

"Is everything all right?" Liese asked. She sat on the couch and patted the cushion next to her. "Sit. Tell me what's happening."

Kasch sat down and ran his hands through his hair, frustrated. "I should just leave this place. Pretend Helmburg never existed."

"What are you talking about?"

"I don't know anymore," he said. "Nothing's been right since I came back. Everyone has lied to me or kept secrets from me or treated me like I don't belong. Everyone except you. You're the only one who made me feel like I could live a normal life here. You're the only one I'll miss when I leave."

"Kasch, you're scaring me. Are you in trouble?"

"Leave with me," he said, surprising himself. He hadn't thought of asking her, but after that the words came rushing out of him in a desperate torrent. "We'll go someplace new, someplace where they've never heard of Luther Möllhausen or the Necromancer or even Helmburg. We can start our lives over, just like you said before, in a house with a stream where we can float paper boats."

The troubled look on her face made his heart sink. "Kasch, you're talking like a madman. I can't do that. I *wouldn't* do that. Helmburg is my home, I don't want to leave it. And if I did, it would have to be for the right person."

The right person. The words were a blade that carved a hollow wound in his chest. Obviously she didn't think he was the right person. That was it, then. There was nothing left for him here, not even Liese. She couldn't help him. Her father couldn't help him. No one could.

He stood up and moved toward the doorway. The coachman had said his broken coach would be ready to go today. Kasch only hoped no one else had claimed it yet.

"Kasch, wait," Liese said, getting up from the couch. "That came out wrong. I didn't mean..." She trailed off with a sigh. "Look, we may have been close as children, but the truth is I hardly know you. The real you, the man you've grown up to be. You've only been in Helmburg a few days. Maybe in time—"

"I'm not staying," he said. "I can't."

"Why?" she pressed. "Why do you have to go?"

He looked at her, and remembered the kiss they'd shared in the tavern cellar as children. They'd been so innocent then, their lives so simple. How could he explain to her now about the suspicious glares, the threats, the rumors about where he came from? He didn't want her to know any of it. He couldn't bear the possibility that she might believe the worst about him too, that she might be frightened of him, even disgusted by him. It would destroy him.

Behind her, a blurry mist appeared. It moved closer, coalescing into a silhouette, and then a body, and suddenly Kasch was looking into a familiar face over Liese's shoulder. A face framed with honey-colored hair.

"Did you really think you could just leave?" the woman from his dream asked.

He trembled, backing up against the wall. How was this possible? How could she be here? He was awake. Wasn't he?

"Kasch?" Liese asked.

He slid down the wall, jamming his fists over his eyes. "Go away! You're not here, you're not real!"

The woman laughed. "Is that what you think?"

Liese pulled Kasch's hands away from his face. "Kasch, stop it, you're scaring me. What's wrong? What's happening?"

"Stay away from me!"

Liese jerked away, confused. "I—I'm trying to help you."

"Don't you see her?" he cried.

Liese turned and looked directly at the woman. "Who? There's no one there. I don't know what's happening, Kasch. I—I think you're still sick from yesterday. I'm going to get help, all right? I won't be gone long. Stay right here. I'll be back soon, I promise."

"Don't go! Please, don't leave me alone with her!" Kasch reached for Liese, but she was already up and running for the door. His arm dropped limply at his side. The phantasm with the face of his mother looked down at him. "You're not real," he said again. Then he laughed. It was surprising how easily laughter came in the face of this lunacy. Or maybe it wasn't that surprising at all. "I'm mad, that's what it is. Something's broken in my head. None of this is real. I'm still in Bern, locked away in a madhouse. Or dreaming in the dorms. Either way, you're just a product of my imagination."

"Am I?" the woman asked. "Don't you know me? After all this time, don't you know me yet?"

Kasch turned away and closed his eyes. "I gave you the face of my mother, but you're not her."

"Mother?" she scoffed. "You have no mother. No father. You were *willed* into existence from dust and bone."

He squeezed his eyes shut harder and felt a teardrop roll down his cheek.

"This game no longer amuses me," the woman said, but her voice had changed, grown deeper. Kasch opened his eyes. A pale young man stood before him now, dark-haired and black-eyed. It took him a moment to realize he was looking at himself. "This is my real face," the other Kasch said. "It is you who wears a false one."

"Wake up!" Kasch cried, and shut his eyes again tightly.

"How adorable, how precious, that you think you can resist me. Especially now, when we're so close to our goal."

Kasch clenched his hands into fists, dug his nails into his palms. "Wake up now!"

But the other Kasch kept talking. "Five assassins walked out of Castle Karnstock alive. Only one remains, and then your work is done." Something heavy landed on floor near Kasch's feet with a metallic clang. "Pick it up."

Kasch opened his eyes and stared at the silver axe on the floor. Its edge was streaked with dried blood. He squirmed, trying to get away from it, but the wall was at his back. There was no place to go. No escape from this.

"Pick it up," the other Kasch ordered. "Finish the job you started. There's only one left."

Kasch shook his head vehemently, cold sweat pooling on his back.

"You shouldn't have tried to leave again. You tested my patience. Forced my hand," his doppelgänger said. "This time you won't have the cover of night to hide behind. This time you won't be able to wash the blood off in the stream behind your house and crawl back into bed. This time everyone will know it was you."

Kasch remembered sitting in the water in his dream, a cloud of tiny red fish floating past him. It hadn't been fish at all. He wriggled, trying to kick the axe away. He fell over and crawled for the door.

"Pick it up!" his own voice thundered in his ear. The other Kasch's lips pulled back in a horrible smile. "I see now. You still don't understand who you are beneath the mask. The truth can be found in blood. Spilled blood. Let the weight of the axe in your hand, and the crunch of bone and meat, tell you your true name."

"God, no. The killer—it can't be me. It can't!"

"Don't resist. Give your will over to me," his doppelgänger said. "Let the two halves become whole."

The room smelled suddenly of ash. Blackness crept into the edges of his vision. He rolled onto his back. He was slipping away, and for the first time he was aware of another presence simultaneously trying to squeeze its way inside him.

"Good boy," said the thing wearing his face.

As the darkness overcame him, he heard the front door open, and a man's voice call out.

Henry Maentel was home.

21.

Walking home from the stable where they'd found Johann's remains, Henry Maentel couldn't shake the images that were stuck in his mind. Clumps of straw in congealed pools of blood. Scattered pieces of flesh and bone. He swallowed hard to keep the bile down.

The handgun tucked into his belt chafed against his stomach. A family heirloom, his grandfather had carved the weapon's ornate ivory grip in the time of Frederick the Great. Henry didn't go anywhere without it anymore. Not while there was a dangerous madman loose in Helmburg.

His meeting with the new Inspector, a promoted constable named Stagg, hadn't gone well. In his estimation, Stagg was an idiot, half the man Barend Lang was. Worse, Stagg refused to release the bodies to the families, who were clamoring for quick burials. The Inspector had read of a new investigative theory out of England and was convinced the remains might still yield more clues. Henry knew he was damned no matter what he did. If he ordered the bodies released prematurely and the murderer was never caught, he'd be blamed for not listening to the Inspector. If he allowed Stagg to delay the burials, he'd anger enough influential families to cost him his position. Either way, his career was over. Helmburg wasn't just slipping through his fingers anymore, it was as good as gone.

Stagg had added insult to injury by devising the ridiculous theory that Edwin, Barend, and Johann had been involved with smugglers and were killed over a black-market transaction gone wrong. The theory would be laughable if it weren't so offensive to the memory of his friends.

He thought of the four wooden spikes in the woods again. This time, he imagined Edwin, Barend, and Johann impaled on three of them. The fourth spike was still empty. Waiting. He knew who for.

Home, Henry stepped into the foyer and closed the front door behind him. "Liese?" he called. "Carla? Is anyone home?"

No one answered. They'd probably gone out, he thought. He should have warned them to stay—

A footstep in the living room made him freeze in place.

"Hello?" he called.

"Father?" a voice replied. "Is that you?"

Henry shuddered. He knew the voice well. Well enough to know it belonged to someone who couldn't possibly be standing on the other side of the living room door.

His dead son Abelard.

Hahn sat at the writing desk by the window of his small flat, staring at the familiar words atop the blank paper before him: *My Dearest Jenelle*. How many times had he tried to write this letter to his ex-wife? It shouldn't be so hard, yet each time he lifted his pen the immense pain of losing their son reared like a startled horse. He wanted to ask Jenelle how she was doing in Versailles, and if she ever thought of him or their boy anymore. He wanted to say he was sorry for the way he'd acted. But she wouldn't want to hear from him, he knew. Not after all this time. His letter would only be reminder of the tragedy they shared.

He crumpled the paper into a tight ball, disgusted, and cursed himself. He was a coward even in the simple act of writing a letter. He threw the wadded-up paper at the wastebasket. It bounced off the rim and landed on the floor. He left it there, a fitting reminder of his failures.

Out his window, he could see the spot on the street where Kasch had collapsed yesterday. Villagers, despite being taxed and scared after the blackbirds attacked, had rushed to help him, but Hahn hadn't. He'd only watched from his window, too frightened to move. Just as he did on Black Easter. Just as he always did.

A frantic knock at the door startled him. He shook his head in disgust. Now he was jumping at his own shadow. Whoever was at the door kept knocking and wouldn't stop. He swiveled toward the door in his chair.

"For God's sake, stop that racket and come in!"

The door burst open, and Liese charged into the flat, out of breath and red-faced from exertion. Her eyes were wide and frightened. "It's Kasch!" she said, struggling to catch her breath. "Something's wrong with him!"

Hahn wanted to rise from the chair, but his body suddenly felt as heavy as iron. "What do you mean? I was with him this morning. He seemed fully recovered."

"I've never seen him like this," she said. "It's like he's gone mad. Please, I didn't know who else to ask. You're his friend and a doctor and I think he might hurt himself."

Hahn's heart sank. He shouldn't have told Kasch those awful rumors. He should have trusted his instincts and left it alone. Clearly, it had been too much for the boy to handle, and now he was lashing out, a danger to himself and possibly others, and it was all Hahn's fault.

Liese was waiting for him to run for the door, but he couldn't move. If he went, what would be waiting for him? A violent, angry boy who would surely see him as the source of all his unhappiness. Whatever injury Kasch was planning to inflict on himself would be turned outward then, aimed at Hahn instead. His fists, a knife, perhaps a bullet...

"Well?" Liese pressed. "Are you coming?"

No, he thought. He should tell her no. If pressed, he would lie so she wouldn't know he was afraid, but his answer would still be no. He couldn't look at her. He looked away, and his gaze fell on the crumpled letter on the floor. A letter he'd started long ago that remained pathetically unfinished even now. He'd filled his sixty-odd years of life with countless excuses for his inaction. Maybe it was time to stop being a coward.

Hahn rose up out of his chair. "Take me to him."

Abelard stood perfectly still in the middle of the living room. Henry Maentel stared at the port-wine stain on the side of his son's face. Tears stung his eyes. He wanted to embrace his boy, he wanted it so badly, but he knew Abelard was dead. His son had died at the Necromancer's hands, and then a second time in the pit. What stood in front of him was a lie.

He'd seen this coming. The fourth spike.

"Why are you looking at me like that?" Abelard asked. The slightest grin creased the boy's face. "Don't you know me, father?"

Henry took a deep breath, struggling not to weaken. This was *not* his son. "So," he said, "you've come for me at last."

"Aren't you happy to see me?" Abelard came closer. "I'm home, father. After all this time, I've come home to you."

Henry's breath hitched. What if he was wrong? What if, by some miracle, Abelard had been returned to him, just as he'd always wished for? But no, he knew better. Had Edwin, Barend, and Johann known too, in their final moments, he wondered? Had they known it was a trick, a mask? He thought he saw a face behind Abelard's face, but then it was gone.

"Is this how you got to the others?" Henry asked. "What faces did you wear for them?"

"I don't understand," Abelard said. He held out his hands. "Please, father."

Henry squeezed his eyes shut. That voice, it was tearing him apart inside. "There is only one who can commune with the dead. Only one who can assume their forms." With a trembling hand, he pulled the handgun from his belt. "It seems Luther didn't finish the job after all."

Abelard's form grew hazy, dissipated into a thick gray mist. "If you know me," a voice said from within the fog, "then you know your weapon can't harm me."

Henry looked at the gun in his hand. "It's not for you," he said.

A figure emerged from the mist, swinging a silver axe. Henry lifted the gun to his temple.

"Hurry!" Liese yelled at Hahn. He was several yards behind her on the street, huffing with exertion even though he was moving slower than a garden snail. She was tempted to pick him up and carry him on her back if it would get them there quicker.

"I'm not as young as I used to be," he replied, out of breath. "If you want my help, you're just going to have to wait for me. How much farther, anyway?"

She grabbed his arm and pulled him forward. "Not much farther. There, see my house? Just over that rise? That's where I left him."

She felt him pull back. She tugged harder. "Quickly!"

"I shouldn't have come," Hahn said. "I'm only holding you up. Please tell me you summoned a constable, too."

"No," she replied. "Kasch isn't himself. He's out of control. I thought a friendly face would be more calming than a truncheon and a jail cell."

Hahn sighed. "Let's hope you're right."

When they reached the house, she opened the front door for him and followed him into the foyer.

"Where did you say he was?" Hahn asked.

She pointed to an open door halfway down the hall. "There, the living room."

Hahn stayed in the foyer and called, "Kasch? It's me, Hahn. Everything's going to be all right. We should talk some more, you and me. About nicer things this time, eh?" There was no reply. "Kasch, did you hear me?" He turned to Liese and said, "He must have left." She hated how relieved he looked. She suddenly understood she'd made a mistake asking Hahn for help. He was a coward, nothing more.

From the living room came the dull thud of something heavy striking the floor.

"Kasch!" Liese ran for the living room, leaving Hahn behind. She skidded to a halt on the other side of the doorway, her mind unable to process the sight waiting for her there.

Kasch stood by the couch in the middle of the room, his face and clothes spattered with blood. His teeth were bared like an animal's, a long line of drool dangling from his bottom lip. He gripped a silver axe in both hands and swung it down again and again as though he were chopping wood. At his feet were sickening chunks of what had once been a human being. An arm, a calf, part of a torso, shreds of clothing stuck to the gore. She thought she was going to be sick.

Hahn came up behind her. "My God," he breathed.

A round object fell free of the mound of body parts and rolled toward her, so covered in blood it left a red trail on the carpet. She followed it with her eyes, transfixed. She didn't know what it was until it hit the leg of an end table and stopped. Then she saw it bore her father's face and the stump of a neck, and she screamed.

Kasch looked up from his work, her scream drawing his attention.

He grinned at her, but the smile was filled with so much cruelty she didn't recognize it. Something dark and cold and alien raged behind his eyes. He stepped toward her with a slow, unstoppable certainty. At her side, Hahn cowered, frozen in place.

"Kasch, don't. Please!" She backed away, realizing too late she'd gotten turned around and was moving away from the door and toward the wall, cornering herself.

He towered over her, raising the axe.

"Don't!" she sobbed. She stumbled over something soft and wet, something she didn't want to see, and fell. She flinched, waited for the blow. "Please!" she screamed. This wasn't Kasch, she told herself. This wasn't the lonely little boy who'd called her Leelee, who'd played hide and seek with her at the tavern when their fathers were together, who'd always hidden in the same spot in the basement. The same spot they'd shared their first kiss. That sweet boy went away a long time ago and never came back. The thing in front of her was only wearing his face.

And then, somehow, she saw him. Kasch was gone, and in his place was a thirteen-year-old boy. He looked exactly as she remembered him. "Leelee," he said. His voice sank into her like a warm tea. He'd come back after all, she thought madly, and driven the bad thing in the Kasch-mask away. She smiled, wiping tears from her eyes. "Don't cry, Leelee," the boy said. "Don't you know me?"

"Yes," she said, laughing with relief. "Yes, I do."

"Remember the games we played?" the boy asked. "I was never scared to hide in the cellar, even in the dark, because I knew you'd find me. You always found me. I want you to be like I was, Leelee. I want you to not be scared."

"I'm not," Liese said, shaking her head and sniffling. "Not anymore."

The boy opened his arms to her. "Then come to me."

She reached for him.

"Kasch, stop!" It was Hahn's voice. She turned and saw the old man's mouth set in a hard, determined line. He took a deep, steadying breath and stepped forward.

She turned back to the boy, but he was gone, the illusion shattered. There was only Kasch as he was now, covered in her father's blood, a crazed look in his eye. He raised the silver axe over his head.

Behind him, Hahn lifted a porcelain vase off the side table. Liese saw Kasch's arms tense. The axe was about to come down on her. With a grunt, Hahn smashed the vase against the back of Kasch's head. The vase shattered, ceramic shards raining onto the carpet. Liese let out a small cry and edged away along the wall, staying low to the floor. Unfazed by the blow, Kasch turned to face Hahn.

"Kasch, listen to me," Hahn said, his voice quavering. "Just put the axe down. We're here to help you. I know you don't want to hurt anyone else."

Kasch paused, studying his face.

"That's right, it's me. Hahn. Your friend."

Liese crawled away from the wall. Her hand touched something sticky on the carpet and came back red. She whimpered. Kasch turned quickly in her direction, his face twisted with rage.

"No, Kasch, look at me," Hahn said. "We're talking. Just us, Kasch. Just you and me."

Kasch turned back to Hahn while Liese crawled away, leaving a trail of smeared handprints behind her. She'd been wrong about Hahn, she realized. He wasn't a coward, he was brave. Braver than anyone. He was a hero.

"Everything's going to be all right," Hahn said. "Just put it down."

The axe moved like lightning. It arced up and came down, slicing deep into the flesh between Hahn's neck and shoulder. The old man grimaced and fell to his knees.

Liese bit back a scream and glanced quickly at the doorway. It was still too far away. She was too deep inside the room, and Kasch was between her and the door. There was no way she could get past him fast enough.

Kasch braced one foot against Hahn's chest and yanked the axe out of him. It came free with a wet sucking sound, and Hahn fell backward. Kasch brought the axe down on Hahn again. Liese turned away quickly. She heard bones snapping, and her gorge rose.

She crawled behind the far side of the couch, praying Kasch wouldn't see her. Her knee touched something on the rug, and when she looked down she had to cover her mouth to keep from screaming. In a small puddle of blood lay a chunk of her father's hand, two fingers and a thumb joined by a wedge of flesh. Then she saw the gun beside it. She picked it up, the blood on the carved ivory handle sticky against her palm.

Kasch's voice startled her. "Hahn?" He sounded groggy, confused. She peeked over the top of the couch and saw him staring at the old man's body. "Where—where am I?"

Liese aimed the gun at him.

Kasch noticed the axe in his hand, the blood all over him, and took a step back. "Oh God, no. I didn't... This—this isn't me." He spun around and saw Liese. The rage she'd seen in his eyes was gone. Now there was only terror and confusion. He walked toward her, the axe still in his hand. "Liese, help me. Please, I don't know what's—"

She squeezed the trigger.

22.

Kasch crouched behind the bushes along the mountain trail. Down in the village below, torches bobbed in the twilight like fireflies. They were looking for him. A band of villagers had already spilled through the gate and started up the mountain. It was only a matter of time before they found him and killed him.

Time wasn't on their side. The bullet Liese had put in his stomach would do the job first. Her gun had held only a single round, and Kasch had managed to stumble out of the house while she screamed and pulled the trigger again and again to the empty clicking of the hammer. He'd run for the Helmburg gate, his life leaking out of him, and soon found himself struggling up the dirt road that led to the mountain pass. He didn't remember having turned onto the side trail, he'd only kept moving until he couldn't move anymore. Then he'd crawled into the bushes, closed his eyes, and waited to die.

He hadn't expected to wake up, but when he opened his eyes the sun was setting, the alarm bell was tolling down in the village, and the search parties had formed. Now, feverish and weak, he turned away from the bobbing torches and took off his shirt, wincing at the sharp, cold pain in his stomach. He balled up the shirt and pressed it against the bullet wound to stanch the bleeding.

The silver, blood-smeared axe lay on the ground beside him. He hadn't realized until now that he'd taken it with him, evidence of his terrible crimes. Maybe death was all he deserved. He crouched lower behind the bushes. His breath came in short, ragged bursts. He tasted something thick and coppery at the back of his throat. It wouldn't be much longer now.

The torches came his way. He heard men calling out to each

other. He backed deeper into the woods, taking the axe with him. If he went far enough into the forest, perhaps they wouldn't find him. Then he could die in peace.

Loud voices made him drop to the ground. Footsteps crunched on the gravelly earth. Two torches bobbed along the trail on the other side of the bushes.

"It's no use," a man said. "The Bürgermeister's daughter says she shot him square in the stomach before he ran off. He couldn't have come this far. We should check the roads below."

"You saw the blood on the trail, Inspector Stagg," the second man said, his angry voice sounding familiar. Kasch lifted his head to peek through a hole in the brush. It was Fritz Gruber, the torchlight reflecting off his bald forehead. "The boy came this way. I can feel it in my bones."

"But there's no more blood to follow," Inspector Stagg answered. "He could have doubled back. If he's not as hurt as the girl thinks, he could be halfway to the next town by now."

"I knew it, right from the goddamn start, when he got kicked out of university for beating on my boy," Fritz growled. "I knew that whore's son would bring nothing but trouble."

Inspector Stagg called to his men to head back down and check the mountain pass to either side of Helmburg. "He's probably dead already," he added. "That should make him easier to find."

"He's not dead," Fritz said. Kasch stiffened, tightening his grip on the axe. Had he been spotted? "And he's not on any goddamn mountain pass," Fritz continued. "He's out there somewhere, waiting to finish the job."

"And what job would that be, Herr Gruber?"

"He killed five people, almost six with the Bürgermeister's daughter. Who knows how many of us that lunatic would have killed given the chance?"

Inspector Stagg sighed, clearly not convinced. "We'll check the roads," he said. "I want to find his body before the wolves do. I need something to show the villagers so they know it's over."

"Over?" Kasch could hear the sneer in Fritz's voice. "Men like that don't die until you put your goddamn hands around their necks. And if he ever comes back, that's exactly what he'll get."

Kasch heard the sound of footsteps again—Fritz and Inspector

Stagg were walking back down the trail. He waited until he couldn't hear them anymore, then stood slowly. His legs shook under him, barely strong enough to keep him upright. He had to keep moving. It was only a matter of time before the Inspector realized Fritz was right and they came back to find him.

The axe grew heavy in his hand, but he refused to drop it. As long as he could feel it there, could feel its weight against his fingers, he was alive. Soon the path became overgrown with grass and weeds. It looked like no one had come this way in years. Loose pebbles slid precariously under his feet. His body weakened with each step, wanting to find a place to lie down and die, but he kept pushing forward. *Just a little farther*, he thought, until he reached a place where they wouldn't find him. *Just a little farther.* Every time he stumbled, he pulled himself up again and forced himself to move. At one point, as the last trace of the sun disappeared beneath the horizon, he fell against a small wooden hutch atop a post, half hidden by overgrown brush on the side of the path. Under the roof was a carving of the Crucifixion, its paint weathered away until Christ and the cross were of the same pale wood, the tortured and the torturer indistinguishable from each other.

He pressed on, fighting the urge to stop and close his eyes, even for a moment's rest. *Just a little farther. Just a little more time.* The moon rose, bathing everything in a ghostly white light. He looked up and saw he was standing before a tall stone wall. There was an archway in front of him, one wooden door hanging unsteadily off its hinge, the other on the ground just inside the doorway. Atop the arch were two great stone axes, crossed like an X.

Castle Karnstock.

He stepped through the doorway and into the courtyard. Around him, black, leafless trees twisted up out of the damp mist that clung to the ground. On the other side of the courtyard were the ruins of the castle. The towers and turrets, parapets and battlements had all collapsed, leaving only a pile of blackened rubble. He could imagine Luther Möllhausen, Edwin Roebling, Barend Lang, Father Johann Vierick, and Henry Maentel rolling flaming barrels of oil into the castle. He could almost see them clearly, translucent figures moving through the courtyard. His mother, too, sitting on a nearby log in her white gown. Their job finished, the figures walked toward the gate. Luther had one arm around his wife's waist. In the other, he carried a silver axe. The same axe with which he'd killed the Necromancer. The same axe Kasch was holding now. Luther had brought it back from the castle, and all the evil and madness had come with it, its shadow stretching across a generation to infect Kasch, even as far away as Bern. He watched the phantoms leave the courtyard, passing through him like a breeze, and then they were gone.

Kasch climbed the front steps of the castle, weaving around fallen chunks of stone and cinder. The doors were gone, the steps leading directly into what was left of a massive hall. Half the ceiling had collapsed, leaving a sloping roof on one side, the other side open to the night sky. Moonlight poured into the room like rain.

At the far end of the hall, Kasch found a big, throne-like chair. In it sat a collection of small, broken, fragmented bones, arranged to form a complete skeleton. The Necromancer's bones. Empty eye sockets stared blindly back at him from the skull that lay tipped back against the chair. Its arms lay draped along the armrests, its fingers resting atop the roaring lion heads carved there.

Welcome home, Kasch.

The voice seemed to come from all around him. The pain in his stomach flared, the bullet biting deeper into his gut. He doubled over, pressing his shirt harder against the wound.

"This isn't my home," he said. "I'm not your son!"

No, you are much more than that.
And so am I.
I have pierced the veil and seen worlds you cannot imagine.
I have lived for hundreds of years in hundreds of places.
Inhabiting new bodies when the old ones wore out.
But this village offered nothing suitable.
I had to create my own.
Conjure a vessel into the womb of a woman.

The pain brought Kasch to his knees. He felt so cold. His legs were numb. "That's a lie," he said through clenched teeth. "Luther killed you before I was even born."

Death is meaningless.
A curtain between two worlds, and parted just as easily.

The pain was excruciating. Kasch doubled over so far his

forehead touched the floor. Blood dribbled from his lips.

Poor, orphaned Kasch.
I am the only one who never abandoned you.
Always within you. Waiting for your return.

Blood-soaked images flashed before his eyes—Edwin Roebling's kitchen, Barend Lang's bedroom, Johann Vierick's stable, Henry Maentel's living room. He saw each of their faces, cowering before him in fear, and the axe in his hands. He could still feel the reverberations of the handle as he'd chopped through muscle and bone.

Even before, you felt me coming through.
All those times your mind went black.
It was my anger you felt, my hatred.
Now, at last, the two halves can become whole.
The time has come to take possession of what is rightfully mine.

Hahn had said life was full of choices and everyone had to live with the choices they made. But Kasch never had a choice. He saw that now. The Necromancer had been manipulating events from the start. All designed to deliver him here. All leading up to this moment.

But the Necromancer hadn't expected him to show up with a bullet in his stomach. Now, just this once, maybe he had a choice after all.

Kasch forced himself back to his feet, but his legs buckled under his weight and he fell again to the hard stone floor. He forced himself up one more time. Just one more minute was all he asked, so he could do this on his feet like a man.

"You're too late," he said. "This body is finished. You won't be able to take me." And with that, he let go. He stopped fighting death's approach and opened himself to it instead, waiting for oblivion to envelope him like a soft blanket.

You misunderstand, Kasch.
I don't need to take you.
I am you.

Kasch reared back, and with his last ounce of strength he hurled the silver axe at the Necromancer's bones. It somersaulted through the air between them, handle over blade, and struck something, and then the bones, the chair, everything shattered. A thousand reflections of Kasch's own face rained down in tinkling shards of silvered glass, and a bronze mirror frame, its corners adorned with the crossed axes of the House of Karnstock, crashed to the floor. The remains of the mirror shattered around his feet.

Kasch laughed, reclining against the tall back of the chair, letting the fingers of one hand play across the carved mane of the lion's head on the armrest. With his other hand, he pulled the shirt away from the bullet hole in his stomach. A thick white liquid seeped out of the wound, carrying the bullet with it. It rolled off his lap and landed on the floor with an inconsequential *tink*. The wound closed, sealed, and was gone.

Slithering shadows in the corners of the ruined castle whispered their welcome. He felt their power flowing through him, filling him, dark and cold and immense.

He'd been foolish to resist for so long. Luther had treated him no better than a dog, abandoning him the first chance he got. The people of Helmburg—Fritz Grubers, all of them—had shown him nothing but suspicion and disdain. Even Liese, the one person he thought would be different, the one person he thought would care, had tried to kill him. But he would have his vengeance. In his mind he saw a vast tidal wave of blood washing over everything, carrying away the boarded-up church, Luther's house, and Huetten's Bierbrunnen, sweeping the villagers from the streets, rolling through Helmburg like an avalanche until there was nothing left but a wet red grave.

The sound of fluttering wings came to him. Above, through the hole in the castle roof, he saw a ribbon of black that stretched across the night sky, obliterating the stars. From far below, the sound of Helmburg's gates closing for the third and final time was almost lost amid the cries of the blackbirds coming home.

END

(F)EARLESS

1.

Kiyoshi Matsushima swiveled his desk chair to face the window in the trailer wall behind him. Outside, a gloomy gunmetal sky had settled over the clearing in Itabashi where they'd set up for the day's shoot. Perfect weather for the scene, really. It was important that everything be perfect. There was a lot riding on this.

That he'd been hired to direct *Seven Chords*, a big-budget movie from a major studio, was nothing short of a miracle, the second chance he'd waited a long time for. Things were about to change for him, he could feel it. They had to. From rock bottom, there was no place to go but up.

The backs of his ears tingled the way they did when he was sure someone was looking at him, and he swung the chair around again.

She stood just inside the doorway, her long, tangled black hair hanging low over her face, obscuring her features save for one milky-white eye that peered out at him through the strands. Her arms hung stiffly at her sides, her skin as pale and thin as onion paper, dark veins visible beneath the flesh. She wore a ratty white dress, filthy from the grave.

"Show me the walk," Kiyoshi said.

She lifted her arms toward him, fingers groping, and took one lurching step forward, then another.

"Stiffer," he said. "Remember, you've been dead for years. Your joints aren't used to moving anymore. And don't show any emotion. Keep your anger, your need for vengeance, on the inside. You're not a woman anymore, you are *yurei*, an angry spirit, a force of nature. Relentless. Unstoppable." She bent her arms slightly at the elbows and wrists, splayed her fingers into claws, and staggered in circles. "Better," he said. His smartphone buzzed, vibrating its way across the desk. He glanced at it, wondering if it was Asumi, his ex-wife, calling about his weekend plans with Mai, but the name on the display was Yasushi Sato, his assistant director. He picked it up and answered, "Yes?"

"Mr. Matsushima? I'm sorry to disturb you, but I'm at the gate." Yasushi sounded tense, agitated, and extremely apologetic. "Shun Takeda is here."

Kiyoshi leaned forward in his chair. "Don't let him in!"

"He already got past security," Yasushi said. "They didn't know he was banned from the set. We're looking for him now, but he's already inside."

"Damn it!" Kiyoshi ended the call, dropped the phone into his pocket, and stood up. Alarmed by his outburst, the actress staggering around the room parted the long hair in front of her face and peered at him through her white contact lenses. Kiyoshi snatched up his clipboard, snapped, "Come on," and led her out of the trailer.

Outside, the autumn air was brisk. He could smell rain on the wind, an approaching storm, and wondered if they could use it for the scene. It could work. Around the set, the crew was up in the trees on ladders and cranes, clearing the remaining leaves from the branches to give the scenery a more sparse, haunted look. Kiyoshi glanced at his watch, then rubbed his forehead. The last thing he needed was Shun Takeda barging in and slowing everything down. He didn't have time for distractions, not on such a tight schedule.

A knot of tension throbbed behind his eyes. He took a deep breath, remembering the coping techniques Dr. Mizuno had taught him. *When you feel it happening, just close your eyes and breathe deeply. Breathe in the good, breathe out the bad.*

When he opened his eyes, the actress in ghost makeup was looking at him expectantly, waiting to be dismissed. He scanned the papers on his clipboard. "We're shooting scenes forty and forty-one, where you come out of the Shakujii River and confront Toshio on the wooden bridge. I'll need you ready in twenty minutes. Tell makeup the veins need to be darker so they show up on film." She ran off toward a cluster of trailers in the distance, the long black hair of her wig billowing at her shoulders.

A man appeared around the corner of Kiyoshi's trailer, dressed in black jeans and a brown turtleneck sweater. His hair was cut short, and he wore thick, black-rimmed glasses. The man froze as he watched the actress run past, then turned angrily to Kiyoshi. "Please tell me *that's* not in the movie!"

Shun Takeda. Kiyoshi made a mental note to fire the security guards.

"*That*," he replied, not bothering to hide the contempt in his voice, "is what the audience wants to see. *That* is what got this movie made, not to mention the American distribution and remake deal. *That* is what got you your money, Mr. Takeda."

"It's a joke, that's what it is," Shun said. "Long-haired ghost women? You can't be serious. It's been done to death. It doesn't even belong in the story. That's not what my book is about!"

"We've been over this before," Kiyoshi said. He looked around for security. Why weren't they dragging this annoyance away already?

"My *book* is what got the movie made, not this..." Shun waved his hand toward the actress as she stepped into the makeup trailer, "this *nonsense*. The book was a number-one bestseller for a reason, Mr. Matsushima, and that reason is that it was new, it was fresh. It wasn't just the same old ghost women coming out of the water. What's next, scary images on a videotape?"

"Don't be absurd," Kiyoshi said.

Shun reached into his coat. Kiyoshi tensed, wondering if the writer was so far gone that he intended to shoot him, but instead Shun pulled out a copy of his book and offered it to Kiyoshi. "Here, take this. Just promise you'll read it. That's all I ask."

"That's what the screenwriter is for," Kiyoshi said. "If you don't like the adaptation, take it up with him. Or with the studio, for that matter."

"I've already tried. No one will return my calls."

Kiyoshi wasn't surprised. He himself had stopped taking Shun's calls weeks ago. "We're on a tight schedule, Mr. Takeda. We've already got a firm release date, we can't go changing everything now."

Shun forced the book into his hands. "Please. You'll see it's better than the script that studio hack wrote. I know you will. You're the director, you have clout. You can talk to the producers, ask them for a rewrite, get them to push the release date back if you need to."

Kiyoshi almost laughed. Like most authors, Shun had no idea how the film industry worked. There was a reason authors were paid so much for the options on their books. It was supposed to shut them up. Furthermore, there was no way he was going to risk rocking the boat just because Shun was unhappy. He needed this job. He needed everything to go smoothly.

Over Shun's shoulder he saw two large men in black shirts jogging toward him, coiled wires dangling from their ears, and he breathed a sigh of relief. Yasushi Sato ran behind them, struggling to keep up, his young face grimacing nervously. When the security guards slowed to a halt behind Shun, Kiyoshi said, "You know you're not supposed to be here. These men will escort you out."

The guards each put a hand on Shun's shoulders.

"I've devoted my life to this story," Shun said, struggling as they tried to pull him away. "You're destroying it!"

"Get this man out of here," he told Yasushi, who nodded breathlessly. Then Kiyoshi added, to Shun, "If you come to my set again, I'll have you arrested."

He turned and started walking toward the camera crew setting up by the bank of the Shakujii River. Listening to Shun's fading threats and cries of indignation as the guards led him away, Kiyoshi glanced at the book in his hand, a manga with a brightly illustrated cover. On it, a spiky-haired boy was wearing earphones and holding an electric guitar as ghostly shapes congregated behind him. Frankly, it looked awful, which made the words INTERNATIONAL BESTSELLER printed across the bottom all the harder to believe. At the top, the title was written in choppy, bleeding *kanji*: EARLESS. *Awful title*, he thought. The studio had been smart to change it.

He tucked the book under his arm and shook his head. Every film had its curse. Sometimes it was an impossible actor. Sometimes it was an incompetent crew. With *Seven Chords*, it was Shun Takeda.

2.

Kiyoshi moved his finger along the Tokyo Metro map on the station wall, tracing the blue stripe of the Mita Line from Itabashi Station all the way to where he lived in Shinagawa Ward. He'd had a car once, but it, like so much of his life before the hospital, was gone now, sold to make ends meet during the dry years after his release when he couldn't find work. His last movie, a yakuza thriller, had to be completed by someone else while he was under Dr. Mizuno's care, but even after he was discharged, even after he assured the producers and studio heads there would be no more breakdowns, his phone didn't ring and his savings drained away. No one wanted to hire a director who'd been in a mental institution. Tracing the line on the map was a ritual he performed twice a day, though he knew the route by heart. It reminded him of all he'd lost, and all he hoped to regain.

As the overcast sky darkened into night, he climbed the stairs to the open-air platform and thought of Mai, his daughter, already twelve years old. He'd missed her tenth birthday while in the hospital, something he still couldn't forgive himself for. It had come shortly after Asumi filed the divorce papers. She refused to bring Mai to the hospital, so he'd been forced to send his birthday wishes over the phone. *Happy double digits, Mai. Daddy loves you. I can't wait to see you again*, he'd said into Asumi's voicemail, praying she would deliver the message. In his darkest hours, it had always been the thought of Mai that kept him from slipping irretrievably into despair, and now, knowing he would have her this weekend, he could feel the stress that had been throbbing behind his eyes start to loosen.

He squeezed between the commuters on the crowded platform,

making his way to the edge. He peered down the tracks, but there was no sign of the train yet. He sighed, uncomfortable. The platform was filled to capacity, a sea of black hair all around him, interrupted only by the occasional headband or hat. The press of their bodies felt like walls closing in on him. It made him think of other walls, bare white walls in a stark eight-by-twelve room, and a window of tempered glass in the door so the doctors could see in...

He forced the thought from his mind. Room 49 was behind him now, a ghost of the past. The wind of an approaching train drew his attention down the length of track again. As the train rounded the bend, its bright headlights dazzled Kiyoshi's eyes. He looked away, blinking, and at the same moment a sudden commotion arose at the far end of the platform. He glanced over, his vision still spotted with floating white dots, and as the train pulled into the station, he thought he saw a single black pant leg extend out from the platform edge. Then, a flash of brown like polished wood, a shape falling onto the tracks. The screams of the people on the platform were indistinguishable from the piercing shriek of the train's emergency brakes. Commuters shoved past him, surging toward the spot where the shape had fallen. He saw people turn away, hiding their faces, and heard the murmur of the crowd as news of a suicide filtered from one end of the platform to the other.

Stunned, Kiyoshi pulled himself together, and took out his phone to let Asumi know he'd be late. But the screen stayed a vacant, indifferent black. The battery was dead. He pocketed the phone again and looked for a payphone, but couldn't find one. There was no way to reach Asumi. He was supposed to meet her and Mai at his apartment. They would leave when he didn't show up. He wouldn't get his weekend with his daughter.

Kiyoshi closed his eyes against the whirlwind building inside him.

Breathe in the good, breathe out the bad. Anxiety is only fear turned inward.

Be fearless.

3.

The entire Mita Line was shut down after the suicide. Kiyoshi's train was replaced with a shuttle bus that crawled through heavy traffic toward Shinagawa. It dropped him off twenty minutes late to meet Mai and Asumi, just as the storm clouds finally opened. He hurried uphill along the narrow sidewalks, holding his briefcase over his head against the cold, pelting rain.

When he reached his apartment building, a reed-thin, three-story structure on a narrow street packed tight with identical buildings, he was surprised to find Asumi and Mai still waiting. His ex-wife stood stiff as a board, holding an umbrella in one fist. Mai, dressed in a yellow rain slicker and matching hat, fussed with the backpack slung over her shoulders and then noticed Kiyoshi approaching. She muttered a feeble, "Hi, Dad."

Asumi fixed him with an icy glare. "You're late. We had to wait in the rain. Mai can't afford to get sick now, not with exams coming up. If she catches a cold..." She trailed off. She didn't need to finish the threat. She was good at not having to finish threats.

"Sorry," Kiyoshi muttered, though what he wanted to say, what he'd always wanted to say, was, *What kind of woman leaves her husband just when he needs his family the most?* But he already knew the answer: one who was ashamed to be married to a man who went crazy.

"Where were you?" Asumi pressed. No answer would be good enough, he knew, but this was how their conversations went now. Insinuations. Lobbed cannonballs of guilt.

"There was a problem with the train," he said, not wanting to frighten Mai with details of the suicide.

With her free hand, Asumi fussed with the collar of Mai's slicker, even though there was nothing wrong with it. "You should have called," Asumi said. "We've been standing here for nearly half an hour. There was plenty of time to call."

"My phone battery died." Saying it out loud, it sounded like a lie.

Asumi straightened. "You know I didn't have to do this, right? My lawyer said I didn't have to, because of what happened, but I said no, I want Mai's father to be in her life. The least you can do is try not to keep your daughter waiting in the rain."

Because of what happened. She meant the hospital. Her lawyer had said she could declare Kiyoshi unfit for visitation because of his breakdown. Not agreeing to it was the last bit of kindness she'd shown him, a scrap of generosity he knew she would hold over his head forever.

"Go greet your father." Asumi gently nudged Mai forward. The girl shuffled over and hugged him lightly, as if she didn't want to touch him. Asumi said, "I'll be back for her Sunday night. Don't let her stay up too late. She has to study for a math exam." She kissed Mai goodbye, then turned and walked to her car.

Kiyoshi put his arm around his daughter, ushered her inside and up the stairs to his apartment on the top floor. It was much smaller than the expensive three-bedroom they'd lived in as a family. That one had been on a floor so high sometimes they could look out the enormous living room windows and see the lamps of the houseboats moored in distant Tokyo Bay twinkling like stars at night. Kiyoshi changed out of his wet clothes and fixed Mai a dinner of fish and noodles.

"You used to take me to restaurants," she muttered, sulking.

"Is something wrong with your father's cooking?" She didn't answer, and they ate in silence until Mai asked about the movie.

"Did you say it was a monster movie?"

"A ghost story," he said.

"Is the ghost a girl with long hair?" Mai asked around a mouthful of fish.

He smiled. "Of course."

Mai rolled her eyes. She yanked her ponytail free of its elastic and pulled her hair down over her face. She stood up, put out her arms, and pranced stiffly around the table. "I'm going to come out of your teeveeeeee," she moaned.

"Sit down and finish your dinner."

Mai tucked her hair behind her ears and sat. "It's so stupid and old."

"It's going to let me take you to restaurants again."

"Why do you like making movies so much anyway?"

He looked up from his plate. "I thought you liked moves."

"But last time…" She trailed off and stole a quick glance at him before staring at her food. He sighed. She knew it was his career that had triggered his breakdown and broken the family apart, she just didn't know how to talk to him about it. She was scared of him, he understood then, and the thought broke his heart.

In his mind, he saw a hallway, institutional cinderblock walls pale green in the light of flickering fluorescent bulbs. At the end of the hall, a door, the number 49 on a brass plate beneath the tempered glass window. This was the kingdom of the mad and the broken, and its king was Dr. Mizuno, who had been so afraid of germs he wore a blue surgical mask around the patients at all times.

"Movies are like moments frozen in time," he told Mai. "You can see things that aren't around anymore, like old buildings and cars. And people, you can see people who aren't around anymore either."

She nodded but still didn't look at him.

"Everything stays the same. If you watch a movie from fifty years ago, everyone still looks young, even if they're old today. That's the real magic of movies, and that's why I like making them. Nothing changes or comes undone. There's always a happy ending."

"There isn't *always* a happy ending, Dad," she pointed out.

"Well, the best stories have a happy ending."

She finally met his eyes. "Does yours?"

For some reason the question was like a heavy stone on his chest, crushing him, and suddenly he felt out of breath. His heart raced. He closed his eyes, calmed himself, and told her to finish her dinner.

Afterward, in the living room, Mai saw him pull the copy of *Earless* from his briefcase and place it on a shelf. She sprang off the couch and snatched it up. "Oh, cool! Are you reading this, Dad?"

"Someone gave it to me today."

"It's my favorite book! All my friends love it, too!"

Kiyoshi grinned. "Oh yeah? Then you're going to love what I'm about to tell you."

But Mai wasn't listening, she was too excited, and he had to admit, it felt good to see her like this. It had been a long time since she'd been anything but sullen. "Oh my God, Dad, you have to read it! It's about this boy who's really good at playing the electric guitar. His name is…um…" She bit her lip.

"Toshio," he said.

Mai flipped through the pages. "No, it's a weird name." She stopped and said, "Ah! His name is Hoichi!"

Kiyoshi frowned. Hoichi? A memory flitted at the edge of his mind. He'd heard the name before. Then it came to him: *Mimi-Nashi-Hoichi*, Hoichi the Earless. In grade school he'd read the story of the blind biwa player whose ballad of the tragic battle of Dan-no-ura attracted the attention of the spirits of dead Emperor Antoku Tenno and his soldiers. But it was the end of the story that had stuck with him. The memory of a ghost tearing off Hoichi's ears had kept him awake at night until his mother, fed up with his constant anxiety, finally convinced him it wasn't true.

"So Hoichi's awesome with the guitar, like *really* good," Mai continued. She jutted out one hip, mimed holding a guitar, and pinwheeled her arm as though strumming the strings. "BAOWW! He writes this song about some old battle that happened in ancient history, and then these ghosts start showing up. Not stupid long-haired ghost girls, these are different. They're like samurai, and an emperor all dressed in robes. It turns out they're the ghosts from the battle he was singing about! Then a Buddhist priest tells him the ghosts are going to kill him, and he paints Hoichi all over his body with, like, these magical words that make him invisible to the ghosts. Except the priest forgets to paint his ears, right? So that's all the ghosts see when they come to get him, and they *rip his ears off* before they leave!" She put her hands over her ears and squealed. "It's so gross!"

Shun Takeda had rewritten the story of *Mimi-Nashi-Hoichi* for a modern audience, Kiyoshi realized, but it had all been changed for *Seven Chords*. The emperor and his soldiers had been replaced with a lone, vengeful female ghost summoned not by the ballad of Dan-no-ura but by mysterious musical notes discovered on a discarded page of sheet music. Even Hoichi's name had been replaced with one the studio thought would be more relatable for a young audience.

"This is what you should make a movie of," Mai said, shaking the manga at him.

Kiyoshi felt lightheaded. "I am. That's the book I'm filming."

"Oh my God!" Mai shrieked, but then her face clouded with confusion, and she flipped through the manga again. "But there's no ghost girl in here. Are you sure this is the right book?"

4.

That night he dreamt of the suicide and woke in the dark, unsure if he'd been stirred from his sleep by the shriek of the train's brakes or a crash of thunder from outside. Rain washed in heavy sheets down his bedroom window, blurring his view of the buildings across the street even as a flash of lightning lit them like a Klieg light. Unable to fall asleep again, he swung his legs out from under the covers. He glanced at the clock on his bedside table. Just past midnight. Damn. His whole night's sleep was shot. A cup of warm tea would put him at ease, he thought. He walked out of the bedroom and into the hallway, and then froze in mid-step.

A shape stood in the kitchen doorway at the far end of the hall, motionless as a statue. He squinted, trying to see in the dark. It was a girl. Her pale arms hung by her sides. Her face was shrouded by a mess of long, tangled hair.

"Mai? What are you doing up?"

The girl didn't move.

A small groan came through the living room doorway beside him. He turned and saw Mai sleeping above the covers on the pullout couch, a tangle of black leggings and an Orange Range concert t-shirt.

Kiyoshi turned to the kitchen again, his heart kicking in his chest, but the doorway was empty. He was seeing things, he told himself. He was half asleep, and his mind was still dreaming.

The phone rang, startling him. Kiyoshi ran back into the bedroom and picked up the cordless by his bed before the second ring, hoping it hadn't disturbed Mai.

It was Yasushi Sato. "I'm sorry to be calling so late, but I don't know if you heard."

"Heard what?"

"So you didn't." Yasushi exhaled loudly. "Shun Takeda's dead."

Kiyoshi sat on the edge of his bed. "What happened?"

"He killed himself. Jumped in front of a train at Itabashi Station. From what I gather, it was quite a few hours after we removed him from the set. I don't know what he was still doing there, but he never went home."

Kiyoshi ran his hand through his hair. He remembered the blur of black and brown leaping off the platform, then thought of Shun's black jeans and brown sweater. He shivered. Without knowing it, he'd witnessed Shun's suicide. "God."

"The funeral's set for Monday afternoon," Yasushi continued. "It would be good if you went. If we all did."

Kiyoshi took a deep breath. "We're shooting Monday. The scene in Toshio's house." He glanced at the empty kitchen doorway, and a sudden sense of *déjà vu* came over him.

"I know there was no love lost between you and Shun, but at the very least it would be good PR to shut down the set early and go to the funeral. He was a popular author, after all. Besides, we can still get a lot done Monday morning. I can make the call time earlier."

Kiyoshi stared at the kitchen doorway, trying to figure out what was nagging at him. Something in the script…

"Mr. Matsushima, are you there?"

"Yes," he muttered. "I'll think about it." He ended the call, opened his briefcase on the small desk opposite his bed, and pulled out a copy of the *Seven Chords* script. He flipped through it until he found the scene they were scheduled to film tomorrow. He sat on the bed, staring at the words.

67. INT. TOSHIO'S HOUSE – NIGHT

A long shot down CORRIDOR, facing KITCHEN DOORWAY. Camera PUSHES IN toward KITCHEN as TOSHIO walks past in foreground holding his GUITAR. Camera continues to PUSH IN, and now we see FEMALE GHOST standing in KITCHEN DOORWAY, silent, unmoving, watching him.

Kiyoshi put the script aside and looked at the empty doorway.

NICHOLAS KAUFMANN

He rubbed his face, and in the dark behind his eyes he saw the pale green hallway again, could almost hear the buzzing of the fluorescent lights.

He couldn't let it happen again. Not now, not after coming so far.

The next day, Saturday, was a disaster. Kiyoshi was edgy and irritable, snapping at Mai over every little thing. By that night, she was demanding to go home. "This is your home," he told her, but she said she hated him and locked herself in the bathroom, because it was the only room in the apartment with a door. When he called Asumi, the smug disdain in her voice when she agreed to pick up Mai a day early sent a jolt of tension along his spine. Sunday morning, Kiyoshi watched from his apartment window as Mai ran out onto the sidewalk where Asumi was waiting. The girl hugged her mother tight and let herself be escorted to the car. Asumi glanced his way and shook her head with stinging disappointment. Mai didn't turn to look at him once.

He thought his shoulders would buckle from the weight of his failures.

5.

Less than half the cast and crew went with Kiyoshi to the vast cemetery outside of Yokohama, where Shun Takeda was to be buried alongside his parents, and yet standing at the grave even their small numbers made up the majority of mourners. Kiyoshi wasn't surprised. Shun was such an arrogant pain in the ass it was easy to imagine him driving away countless friends and family members in his lifetime.

It made him think of Mai. He'd tried to call her that morning before school. Asumi had answered. *I think it would be for the best if you two took a break for a while,* she'd said, though he knew what she meant was, *There's still something wrong with you. They let you out too soon.*

As the priest chanted, Kiyoshi pulled his coat tighter against the chill. A photograph of Shun, unsmiling and severe behind his black-rimmed glasses, hung on the face of the gravestone. Kiyoshi couldn't take his eyes off it. He'd watched Shun die. It had happened right in front of him.

Why was Shun still in Itabashi at that hour? Why had he stayed?

After the service, Kiyoshi remained by the graveside while Yasushi went ahead to get the rented limousine. A bearded man in a crisp, charcoal-gray suit separated from a group of mourners and approached him. "It was good of you to come, Mr. Matsushima," the man said, bowing. "Kenjiro Nagahama. I'm the artist Shun worked with on *Earless.*"

"Good to meet you," Kiyoshi said. He turned back to the gravestone.

Kenjiro sighed. "Shun was always a deeply troubled man. Obsessive. Demanding."

"Tell me about it."

To his surprise, Kenjiro laughed. "It's no secret Shun loathed you. That you came to pay your respects goes a long way."

"Whatever issues he had with me, he's at peace now," Kiyoshi said.

"That would be a first," Kenjiro said. "But no, he took his own life in anger and despair. I have a hard time believing his spirit is resting well."

"You don't really believe in ghosts, do you?"

"I believe in a lot of things, Mr. Matsushima. Don't we all, at funerals? We wish the deceased a peaceful rest. We pay our final respects. On a day like today we all believe in spirits."

Kiyoshi studied the photograph on the gravestone. Shun stared back at him. "He must have been difficult to work with."

"You have no idea," Kenjiro said. "Shun was a perfectionist. If he wasn't in complete control, it infuriated him. He stood over every panel I drew and pointed out everything he thought I was doing wrong. Any mistake, any deviation from his vision, and he would explode and insist I was destroying his story. There were some panels I had to draw nearly a hundred times before he was satisfied. To Shun, the legend of Hoichi was everything. Did you know Shun had a degree in folklore?" Kiyoshi shook his head. "He was obsessed with *Mimi-Nashi-Hoichi*. He devoted his life to studying and interpreting the legend. It became his world. He was convinced the old legends of Japan were being forgotten by each new generation, in danger of being lost forever and replaced with what he called the empty totems of pop culture. It was his idea to reinterpret the story of Hoichi as a manga that would appeal to the younger generation. And it paid off. *Earless* was extremely successful. It made both our careers, and he actually seemed happy for a time, until the movie deal happened."

"Why didn't that make him happy, too?"

"Control issues, remember? The publisher owned the movie rights, but if he'd had his way, there probably never would have been a movie. Especially not yours. He hated what you were doing to the story."

"It would have made him a rich man," Kiyoshi said.

"He was already rich. What he valued was artistic integrity.

What he wanted was respect." Kenjiro bowed again. "Good luck with the movie, Mr. Matsushima. I hope it does well for you."

Kiyoshi watched him walk away, then made his own way down the narrow paved path that cut through the cemetery. In the distance, Yasushi waited by the limousine. Kiyoshi walked toward him as the cold wind picked up, biting through his coat and blowing leaves across the ground.

The backs of his ears tingled. He turned, certain someone was watching him, and noticed a woman standing atop a low hill in the distance, shadowed by a leafless tree. The wind rustled the long, tangled black hair in front of her hidden face. Her white dress was torn and dirty, her pale hands bent into claws. At first he thought it was the actress playing the ghost in *Seven Chords*, that for some reason she'd come to the funeral still in her wardrobe and makeup, but then he remembered that she'd taken the day to visit her parents in Nagoya. She hadn't come with them at all. Kiyoshi's mouth went dry.

The woman didn't move. A shape crested the hill behind her and stood at her side. It was another pale woman in a filthy dress, identical to the first. Together they stared at him from behind their hair.

Kiyoshi hurried to the waiting limousine. He dove into the back seat and pulled the door shut. He risked a glance through the tinted window, jabbed his thumb in his mouth and bit down hard, but they wouldn't go away; they kept watching him from beneath the tree. He heard blood rushing in his ears. Heard the slam of the door of Room 49.

Yasushi got in beside him and caught the look in his eye. "Are you okay?"

"Fine, fine. Let's just go."

6.

Kiyoshi was on edge all the next day on set. The sight of the actress in her dirty dress and ghost makeup put a ball of ice in his stomach. He snapped at everyone, actors and crew alike, and by the end of the day they were averting their eyes and talking in hushed tones. He felt like a bomb waiting to explode.

He bought a newspaper to read on the train ride home, hoping it would help him relax. Finding a seat on the crowded train, he leafed through the paper, skimming listlessly through political reports and sports scores until he came across Shun Takeda's obituary. Each word he read shortened the bomb's fuse. Shun had attended Hokkaido University as a folklore scholar. He never wrote another manga after *Earless*. Rarely did public events or signings. Didn't marry, had no children. Lived alone in Shimonoseki.

One line in particular jumped out at him: *The reclusive author created the internationally bestselling manga with illustrator Kenjiro Nagahama, a Buddhist priest turned artist.*

Kenjiro was a priest? He hadn't mentioned it at the funeral.

Kiyoshi glanced at the passengers packed in around him, holding onto the handles above their heads and swaying with the movement of the train. A cluster of commuters was gathered around a pole in front of him, jostling for space, and through the hive of shoulders and scarves he saw a long cascade of black hair. He stiffened, the newspaper crumpling in his hands. Then he saw it was only a woman with her head bent over a book, and he let out his breath.

Home, he ate a quick dinner and settled in front of the television to watch the dailies he'd burnt to DVD. He wasn't expecting to see anything good, the whole day had been a waste, but he figured focusing his mind on something would help calm him. He slipped the disc into the player and turned on the set.

The screen filled with static. He hit the Fast Forward button on the remote, and still saw only static. "You're kidding me," he said, annoyed. The static cleared away suddenly to reveal black-and-white footage of a man, his back to the camera, standing at the bottom of the steps to Itabashi Station. Kiyoshi leaned forward on the couch. "What the hell?" He hadn't shot any of this footage.

The man turned around and glanced into the distance, as if he were looking for something. Kiyoshi squinted at the screen in confusion.

It was Shun Takeda.

Shun climbed the steps to the platform, walked to one end, checked his watch. A train came and left, and still Shun remained, waiting for something. Kiyoshi hit the Fast Forward button. More trains arrived, departed; crowds swelled on the platform and then drained into the doors; the sky grew progressively darker; and all the while Shun waited. Then, Shun's expression turned angry as something in the crowd caught his attention. Kiyoshi scanned the commuter's faces, trying to find what Shun had seen, and he caught a glimpse of—

Himself.

He was the one Shun had been waiting for. That was why Shun had stayed in Itabashi. He'd *wanted* Kiyoshi to witness his suicide.

The image on his TV flickered, jumped, and Itabashi Station disappeared. In its place was a cinderblock corridor, lit from above by flickering fluorescent tubes, and at the end of the hall, a door marked 49.

Then static again. Kiyoshi watched it drift across the screen like snow. He tried to remember the coping techniques Dr. Mizuno had taught him, but suddenly he couldn't. After a minute, he managed to get off the couch and turn off the TV. He removed the DVD carefully, afraid to touch it. Written in black marker across the top, in his own handwriting, were today's date and the scene numbers they'd shot. Impossible. Where had the images come from? How had they gotten on the disc?

It plagued him well into the night, keeping him from sleep. When he did finally drift off, a loud crash in the bedroom woke him immediately. Terrified, he glanced around the room and thought he saw a ragged shape moving through the darkness, but when he worked up the courage to switch on the bedside lamp his room was empty.

He sprang out of bed and searched the room, but there was nothing. He felt like a fool. He had to pull himself together. There was too much at stake to let himself come undone now.

Through the window, movement caught his eye. Two women stood in the street below. Long, tangled black hair hid their faces, but he knew they were looking at him. Another woman, identical to the others, walked stiffly out of the shadows to join them, and then there were three staring up at his window.

7.

The phone was ringing. It had been ringing all day. Kiyoshi sat at the dining table with his knees drawn up to his chest. He couldn't answer the phone because the phone was in the bedroom, and so was she. She'd been standing by his bed when he woke in the morning, wild black hair hanging over her face.

This wasn't another breakdown. He knew that now. This was all Shun's fault. It had started with Shun's death, the suicide he'd forced Kiyoshi to witness. The writer's angry spirit was haunting him.

The phone stopped ringing. How many calls did that make now? Five? Six? He could guess who it was: Yasushi Sato, wondering why he wasn't on set. Had Yasushi called the studio yet? Was there already an angry message threatening to take him off the movie? *We shouldn't have hired you, Mr. Matsushima. They let you out too soon.* He couldn't let them do that. *Seven Chords* was all he had left.

Kiyoshi rose from the chair and peered down the hall toward his bedroom doorway. The room beyond looked quiet. He crept closer, desperate not to make a sound. If she heard him, she would come to the door and stare at him from behind her hair, and he couldn't handle that, he just couldn't. He peeked slowly inside the room, and found it empty.

He sat on the bed, picked up the cordless, and dialed his voicemail. A half-dozen messages from Yasushi clogged his mailbox, ranging from annoyed to concerned. Kiyoshi figured he should call him, tell him to send everyone home. He could make up an excuse why he wasn't there—a cold, a migraine, anything but the truth. No one would believe him. He'd be sent back to Room 49, but this time they'd be wrong. This time it wasn't his fault.

He was about to dial Yasushi's number when the phone rang in his hand. The display showed Asumi's name. Why was his ex-wife calling him? He hit the Talk button. "Asumi?"

Only static answered him.

"Mai?" Kiyoshi sat up straight. More static. "Mai, is that you?"

He thought someone spoke then, but he couldn't hear what they said. Long strands of black hair had begun to push out of the tiny speaker holes at the top of the phone. The hair kept flowing out, dangling lower, lower. It touched his hand, dry and brittle like straw, and brushed against the sensitive skin of his wrist.

Kiyoshi screamed and dropped the phone. He scuttled backward and fell off the bed, knocking a pile of papers off his desk. Something heavy dropped onto his hand. The copy of *Earless* Shun had given him. Hadn't he put it on the shelf in the living room? How had it gotten into his bedroom? The book had fallen open, he saw, its two halves straddling his fingers like a tent. He picked up the manga, his thumb slipping between the open pages, and turned it over.

The page where it had fallen open showed only a single panel of a hand holding a telephone. Thick, gooey ectoplasm oozed out of the handset and down the character's arm. Kiyoshi glanced at the phone he'd dropped. The hair was gone. Then he looked again at the almost identical scene on the page.

Kiyoshi thought of what Shun said as he'd put the manga in his hands: *Just promise you'll read it. That's all I ask.* Was that what this was about? Was that all Shun's spirit wanted of him, to read the book?

Taking it into the living room, he sat with his legs crossed on the couch, a cup of hot tea on the coffee table to soothe his nerves, and read *Earless* front to back, taking in Shun's words and Kenjiro's artwork. The story was just as Mai had described it, and filled with details Kiyoshi remembered from when he'd read the legend of Hoichi as a boy. He stopped when he turned a page and saw a ghostly samurai standing in a doorway at the end of a long corridor, just like the first ghost woman Kiyoshi had seen. His pulse quickened. He read on, and soon came across a panel where two spirits dressed as samurai watched Hoichi from a cemetery hilltop, beneath the shadow of a leafless tree. His hands trembling, he kept reading, and stopped again when he saw Hoichi looking out the window of his apartment at night. Three spirits, the one in center dressed in the regalia of an Emperor, stood on the street below, staring up at him.

Kiyoshi turned the page and nearly dropped the book. There, in crisp black ink, was Hoichi, sitting cross-legged on his couch and reading a book exactly as Kiyoshi was, a cup of tea in exactly the same place on the coffee table. A box of text in the corner of the panel revealed what the boy was reading: *Hoichi, with the holy sutra painted across his body to keep him invisible to the spirits, heard the ghostly samurai's rage at not being able to find him. Suddenly he felt his ears gripped by fingers as cold and hard as iron, and torn from his head. Great as the pain was, he gave no cry to alert the spirit to his presence. As the heavy footfalls receded and vanished, Hoichi felt warm, thick blood trickling from where his ears had been. The only places on his body where the priest had forgotten to paint the sutra.*

The end of the manga was the same as the legend, Hoichi losing his ears to the ghosts. That, too, had been changed for the movie. In the *Seven Chords* script, Toshio sacrificed himself to stop the vengeful ghost from killing his friends, electrocuting himself with a faulty guitar amp. Kiyoshi closed the book and looked again at the cover illustration of the teenage guitarist. Only now did he notice the slight trickle of blood coming out from under the boy's earphones.

Was that enough? Would the haunting end now because he'd read Shun's manga? Or did Shun want him to admit the book was better than the script?

"It is," he said to the empty room. "You were right. It's better."

The room stayed silent. Nothing moved. No hair grew out of his tea, no ghost women emerged from the cracks in the walls. Maybe it was over. Maybe that was all Shun had needed to rest in peace.

But that night, as Kiyoshi slept, it became clear nothing was over. He dreamt of the suicide again, only this time it was he himself who leapt in front of the oncoming train. A platform full of ghostly women watched him, crowded together like a sea of long black hair. When he woke, his heart was pounding in his chest like he'd just run a marathon, and he understood.

Shun Takeda wanted him dead.

Frustrated, Kiyoshi flipped through *Earless* again. If the manga was so important to Shun, the answer had to be in there somewhere. He'd simply missed it the first time through. He turned page after page and paused when he reached Hoichi's meeting with the Buddhist priest. Kiyoshi looked closer and realized Kenjiro had drawn his own face on the priest. An inside joke, he figured, a reference to the fact that the illustrator had once been a Buddhist priest himself.

And suddenly Kiyoshi knew what he had to do. He jumped off the couch and ran for the phone.

8.

Kenjiro opened the door of his small house, frowned at Kiyoshi, and said, "You look terrible."

"He won't let me sleep," Kiyoshi said. "He won't give me a moment's peace." He followed Kenjiro into the living room. All the furniture had been pushed to the walls, he noticed, and a large bamboo mat and six clay bowls had been set up in the middle of the room.

Kenjiro motioned for him to sit on the mat. "I'm not surprised. Bad dreams, hallucinations, spirits have the power to get inside your head and make you see what they want you to see."

Kiyoshi thought of the train ride he'd taken on his way to Kenjiro's house. Ghostly, long-haired women had stood on every platform they passed. "I didn't think you would believe me."

"I told you, I believe a lot of things. When Shun took his own life, he was furious at you, and that fury still burns inside him." He sat across from Kiyoshi on the mat and picked up a tapered horsehair brush from the floor beside the bowls.

"He wants to kill me," Kiyoshi said.

"Anger is all he knows now. But I think I can help you." Kenjiro picked up one of the bowls. A viscous black liquid swirled inside. He dipped the brush into it. "Remove your clothes."

Kiyoshi unbuttoned his shirt. "You're sure this will work?"

Kenjiro smiled. "It worked for Hoichi, didn't it?" He moved the brush to Kiyoshi's chest and painted a small *kanji* there, then another. The ink was cold against Kiyoshi's skin.

"But it's not true, is it?" Kiyoshi asked while Kenjiro continued painting. "The legend of Hoichi, I mean?"

Kenjiro shrugged, squinting at his work. "Who's to say whether a legend is true or not? All that matters is that it's told, and remembered. Shun understood that more than anyone."

Kiyoshi glanced around the floor but didn't see any scrolls or sheets of paper for Kenjiro to work from. "You know the sutra by heart?"

"I was a Buddhist priest for many years. The *Hannya-Shin-Kyo* was drilled into us."

Kiyoshi chuckled. It felt good to laugh again. "I've never heard of a priest becoming a manga artist before."

Kenjiro sighed. "Money can make you do strange things. My family was poor and needed help. As a priest I couldn't earn money to send back home, but with my art I could. So I left the priesthood, and before I knew it a dozen years had passed and I had built a career. I never went back."

"I'm sorry."

"We all make sacrifices," Kenjiro said. "We do what we can to help others. It's why I became a priest in the first place."

Painting the sutra over his body was a painstaking process. Kiyoshi sat, and at times stood, perfectly still, trying to ignore the humiliation of his nakedness. Kenjiro drew letter after letter over him, each one abutting the next so that no patch of skin went uncovered. "And your ears," he said as Kiyoshi felt the pointed tip of the brush dab his earlobe. "We don't want to make the same mistake Hoichi did. There, now we just have to wait for the ink to dry."

"And then?" Kiyoshi asked.

"Then you'll do as Hoichi did. Go home and wait for Shun to come again tonight."

Kiyoshi looked at his painted arms, the thick black *kanji* of the sutra bending and warping over his muscles and bones. He touched his face, felt the sticky ink on his cheeks and forehead. "I can't ride the train home like this."

Kenjiro retrieved a keyring from one of the tables against the wall. "You can borrow my car. When you get home, sit perfectly still, no matter what you see or hear. In order for this to work, you mustn't make eye contact with Shun, and under no circumstances should you speak, even if he demands it."

Kiyoshi looked at his own painted chest. Suddenly, it all seemed absurd. "You're sure he won't be able to see me?"

"Absolutely," Kenjiro said. "If he can't find you, his anger won't have a focus and his spirit will move on. I promise you, by tomorrow morning this will be over."

The sun was setting by the time the ink dried. Kiyoshi thanked Kenjiro and took the artist's car. As he drove, he saw the letters upon his hands on the steering wheel, caught glimpses of them on his face in the rearview mirror, and wondered what he was doing. Was a dead man really haunting him? The hallucinations, the nightmares, he'd experienced them before without the luxury of believing an angry spirit wanted him dead. He pulled to the side of the highway and rested his head against the steering wheel. How had he let this happen? How had he slipped so far into madness without realizing it? No wonder his marriage had crumbled. No wonder his daughter wanted nothing to do with him.

After a few minutes, he gathered himself and pulled the car back into traffic. It was already dark when he arrived. He opened the door and stepped into a hallway of plain cinderblock walls and a hard cement floor. Fluorescent lights hummed along the ceiling, casting a greenish tint on his surroundings. At the far end of the hall, an open door waited for him, and beyond it he saw the bare plaster walls and stark wooden furniture of Room 49.

He took a deep breath and tried to breathe out the bad. There never should have been a Room 49. Not those numbers together. *Shi* and *ku*. Death and agony.

And yet, even after Dr. Mizuno had discharged him, Kiyoshi always knew he'd be back one day.

The cement floor was no longer bare. Now it was covered with a brittle mat of long black hair that crunched and rolled under his feet.

It wasn't real, he told himself. Nothing he'd seen was real. It was only his anxiety, his fear turned inward.

Be fearless.

As he walked toward his room, he peeled off his clothes. He didn't deserve them. They were the clothes of a man, and he was not a man. He was a failure. A failure as a filmmaker. A failure as a husband. A failure as a father. Naked at the end of a trail of discarded clothing, he sat in the middle of Room 49 and listened to the familiar click of the door as it closed behind him. To one side was the narrow, wood-framed bed he remembered. To the other, the scrubbed metal sink and toilet. Before him, the comforting blank whiteness of the wall. This room, more than anywhere else, was where he belonged. Kenjiro had told him to go home, and so he had.

The backs of his ears tingled. Someone was behind him. He hadn't heard the door open. He turned and saw a man standing by the door. Kiyoshi turned away quickly, ashamed. "Hello, Dr. Mizuno."

"I was hoping I wouldn't see you back here," Dr. Mizuno said. His footsteps drew closer. "What have you done to yourself?" A hand touched Kiyoshi's shoulder. The fingers felt cold, spongy. Latex gloves. Dr. Mizuno and his germ phobia. "Are these words? *Hannya-Shin-Kyo*," he read off Kiyoshi's skin. Then he laughed. "The holy sutra? Am I to call you Hoichi now?"

Kiyoshi shuddered at the name, and at the doctor's probing touch.

"You shouldn't have let it get this bad before coming to see me," Dr. Mizuno continued. "I read with some concern about you directing another movie. I warned you to find another line of work, didn't I? Something that wouldn't set you off again?"

Kiyoshi was too ashamed to answer.

"I can't help you if you won't talk to me," Dr. Mizuno said. "Why did you take this film, after everything we discussed? Why, when you knew the risk, would you undo all the work we did together?"

He thought of Asumi calling the hospital to tell him she was leaving him. He thought of Mai saying that she hated him. "To prove that I could," he said.

"Prove to whom?"

"Mai, Asumi, the studios. Everyone."

Dr. Mizuno came around from behind and squatted before him, his white doctor's coat billowing out over his knees. A blue surgical mask covered the lower half of his face. "No, that's not it."

"No one wanted me when I left here," Kiyoshi said. "Not the studios, not my wife, not my own daughter. Everyone thought I was crazy."

"Are you?"

"No," he insisted. "But something's wrong with me. I've been seeing things."

"Was it worth it?" the doctor asked. "Taking this stupid movie that wouldn't even be as good as the book? Was it worth it to be so selfish, so stubborn?"

Kiyoshi glanced up, met Dr. Mizuno's eyes, and saw only cruelty there.

"You didn't do it for anyone but yourself," Dr. Mizuno continued. "You wanted to show everyone, no matter what the cost. You brought this on yourself."

"That's not true," Kiyoshi insisted. "Directing is the only thing I've ever been good at. It's all I know how to do. What choice did I have?" But even as he said it, he knew it wasn't the whole truth. What he'd wanted was for everything to go back to the way it had been before the first breakdown. For everything that had come undone to be mended, all the cuts in his life spliced back together, his career, his family. He thought there could be a happy ending.

"You're pathetic," Dr. Mizuno said. "You're a liar and a coward."

Kiyoshi blinked back tears. "Why are you talking to me like this?"

Dr. Mizuno stood, shaking his head with disgust. "You think you're an artist? You're a hack. What do you understand of artistic integrity? What do you know of the sacrifices an artist makes for his art?"

"You're supposed to be helping me," Kiyoshi said. Dr. Mizuno started walking toward the door, out of Kiyoshi's line of sight.

"There's no salvation here," Dr. Mizuno said. Kiyoshi heard the snap of the doctor pulling off his latex gloves. "Kenjiro warned you not to speak. You should have listened."

Kiyoshi stiffened.

The walls of Room 49 melted away, and he saw his own living room around him. When the man behind him spoke again, it wasn't with Dr. Mizuno's voice.

"No more rewrites, Mr. Matsushima. No more long-haired ghost women. The empty totems of pop culture have no place here. *This* is how the story goes. And this is how it ends. This is how it always ends. Nothing is more important than that."

Hands as cold and hard as iron gripped Kiyoshi's ears, and began to pull.

ABOUT THE AUTHOR

Nicholas Kaufmann is a critically acclaimed author of horror and dark fantasy whose works have been nominated for the Bram Stoker Award, the Shirley Jackson Award, and the Thriller Award. He lives in Brooklyn, NY with his wife and two ridiculous cats. Visit his website at nicholaskaufmann.com.

Curious about other Crossroad Press books?
Stop by our site:
http://store.crossroadpress.com
We offer quality writing
in digital, audio, and print formats.

Enter the code FIRSTBOOK
to get 20% off your first order from our store!
Stop by today!

CPSIA information can be obtained
at www.ICGtesting.com
Printed in the USA
LVOW09s1311200318
570501LV00013B/272/P